D1177629

The Tenants were Corrie and Tennie

a novel by

Kent Thompson

Macmillan of Canada / Toronto
St. Martin's Press / New York

The Tenants were Corrie and Tennie

Published simultaneously in Canada by

The Macmillan Company of Canada Limited
70 Bond Street, Toronto, Ontario M5B 1X3

ISBN 0–7705–1001–9

and in the United States of America by

St. Martin's Press, Inc.
175 Fifth Avenue, New York, N.Y. 10010

Library of Congress Catalog Card Number 72–90482

Printed in Canada

To Michaele

An idea is not responsible for the man who holds it.

Adapted from a saying by Don Marquis

One

I bought the house because I wanted it.

It is a duplex — a frame building with grey shingle siding, trimmed in white. The white sets off its lines rather nicely, I think. It is not an impressive building, but it has an air of being both graceful and substantial.

It was built in 1938 by the previous owner, James Secombe, who lived in it with his wife, Sarah, until he sold it to me and retired to live in Gator Springs, Florida. He worked for the Canadian Pacific Railway until he retired.

In order to buy the house I had to take an 8½ per cent private mortgage. James Secombe holds the mortgage, and to avoid complications, I pay my mortgage directly to the Bank of Montreal here. I act as his agent and pay the tax to the Receiver General of Canada every month. Then I deduct the tax I have paid to the government (it is computed at the rate of 15 per cent of the monthly interest payment) and send a cheque to the Bank of Montreal to be deposited to Mr. Secombe's account. In the summer he will return to Canada to draw in a breath of fresh air and spend the money I have paid into his account. When I bought the house I thought that 8½ per cent was a very high mortgage to pay. Now, it seems, it is a cheap mortgage. In fact, I know very little about such things.

However, I know more than you suspect.

I simply wanted the house. It stands on the corner of Howard and Rodman streets, and you would have to drive out of your way and forsake the main drag (in this area, Regent Street) if you wanted to see it. The corner it stands on is not a particularly busy corner except at 5 o'clock in the evening when several cars stop by at the combination soda pop/grocery store across the street—it is called The Stop Shoppe—so that the drivers may make purchases therein. The little shop also sells a very good French bread, baked on the premises, which is excellent when served hot with ground-up cheddar cheese and a little onion salt.

The duplex is of course two storeys high. It is divided in the middle, so the two units are side by side rather than top and bottom—which is sometimes the case with so-called "duplexes" advertised here in Fredericton. *Such* buildings, however, although they may be perfectly comfortable, always strike me as being upper and lower *apartments.* This is not the case with my house. My house has a left side and a right side, and both sides have front and side entrances and basements.

I think that in many ways my house is a very pretty house, with its sedate grey and its white trim, stretching out gracefully under the maple trees. It is genial; proportionate; in tune with time. There is one red oak in the back yard of my half of the house.

I saved my money for a long time in order to be able to buy such a house, although I did not do so with any deliberate intent or forethought. But when I found out that it was for sale I imagined myself sitting on the long glassed-in verandah in the autumn, watching the leaves fall, and I thought: "That's for me." I could imagine how the leaves would smell when they were damp in the early autumn, and how, later, they would scratch ever so lightly on the sidewalk when they turned dry and crisp.

But I particularly wanted to buy a duplex because I wanted an income property as well as a refuge, and a duplex seemed to fit both needs. Indeed, it enabled me to stop teaching school long before I reached the usual retirement age – although I don't complain about my years as a schoolteacher because, oddly, I learned a great deal from them, and besides, it did not take me long to learn how to insulate myself from the pupils. I treated the children as part of my job, and things went along. Not merrily, but not badly.

Then one day I was in Fredericton (the Chippewa Tourist Service Green Line Tour of the Maritime Provinces of Canada), and I decided to stay. I explained to the driver that I was going to stay (he was perplexed and said that nothing like this had ever happened in his experience and I realized of course that there would be no refund), and I moved out of the Lord Beaverbrook Hotel to much humbler quarters in the Windsor Hotel. I enjoyed that gesture.

But in an odd way I had prepared for it, and could even well afford it. Which is to say that I had been saving money at a steady if unexceptional rate for fifteen years, and there it was. My pleasures have always been so few – good books (readily available at a library), and a cup of percolated coffee with a dollop of Tia Maria in it and – my one luxury – whipped cream. One cannot expect life always to be exciting; one can at best hope that it will not be unfortunate or unhappy. And gradually, simply by living that life which I chose to live, the money accrued, the opportunity arose, and I was free as a man could hope to be.

I have not been miserly. When I have needed things I have bought them, with no undue attention to the price, although without any carelessness, either. Usually I have purchased my clothing at Sears (Simpsons-Sears in Canada) and I have found that I have received good value for my money. Your experience may not be the same. However, I never opened a charge account. I have carried a simple and straightforward savings account at one of the banks in the areas where I have lived, and I have drawn the usual percentages of interest. I have never been tempted to make my money make money. I have never invested in stocks, for example, nor even in bank bonds or government bonds. I have banked my money and ridden the various economies with all the stolid acceptance of a careful sailor cruising the more sheltered areas of the sea.

But when I saw this duplex and realized that it was for sale, I saw the opportunity to snug-in for my remaining years. Because I had sufficient capital to offer quite a substantial down payment, my monthly payments are not very heavy. And my tenants, therefore, who will be paying a very good rent, will provide me with my own necessary income. They will be buying the house for me, and the house will provide my own necessities for shelter. I am not noting the exact figures, however (perhaps you've noticed), because I feel that such notes are dangerous.

Living is a wary art — I learned that a long time ago — and it was about the time that I learned that that I learned that certain superstitions (even "folk" sayings) are important. If they do not indicate any great profundity, they none the less often reflect a worthwhile piece of advice. It was my mother who told me — she was old by the time I was born, and consequently was something of a grandmother to me — that one should never reveal exact figures to anyone.

"They get hold of you by the numbers," she said. It is good advice.

I bought the house in this way: I had noticed an empty duplex at the other end of Rodman Street, and I had stopped at the Stop Shoppe to ask if anyone there knew if it was for sale. There was an old fellow there, buying his evening paper. "The one you're talking about is not for sale," he told me. "But the one over there – that big grey shingle with the white trim – that one's for sale for ready money." He knew old Secombe, he said. I did not ask him for further particulars, although he seemed ready enough, even eager, to talk.

I simply walked across the street to the house. Secombe was out in front, pushing his lawnmower. He was a spare man with a lined face, and he looked to me like a man who held definite opinions. I asked him if it was true that his house was for sale. He replied that it was if the right buyer came along. We talked longer and it turned out that there were several small factors to be considered in the negotiations. First: ready money. Second: the right price. And third: another buyer. Not surprisingly, he did not present them in that order. He simply mentioned that another fellow was interested in buying the place – "mostly for the land. Land-values are up now, you know" – and that this fellow was ready to offer him cash. I told him that I was interested, and I went downtown to have a dinner and think on the matter. It seemed to me unlikely that the other fellow would come up with the sufficient amount of cash.

As I ate my dinner at the Paradise Gardens Restaurant, I allowed myself to think about the house, and it was then that I imagined myself sitting on the glassed-in verandah watching the leaves blow and swirl about in that curious golden light of early autumn. I decided that I wanted the house; no doubt about that. And I revelled in the thought that I could live in the house in comfort for the rest of my life. Life on a deep feather bed until the final moment: the call of death.

Yet, I did not then allow myself to become too excited. I am a thinker of second thoughts. Indeed, I pride myself on my second thoughts. They are protective, and above all, I think of myself as a survivor. The problem of life—then—was simple: how to survive in the best way possible. If "the best way possible" meant wearing bib-overalls the rest of my life, I was prepared to accept that. You who are similarly given to second thoughts will notice, of course, that the difficulty in dealing with the simple problem lies in the definition of "the best way possible". I found myself smiling at the problem in the same way that I sometimes smiled when my pupils grappled with some elementary proposition which was difficult only because it was unfamiliar. For them the unfamiliar was as difficult as the difficult. Do you follow that?

I returned the next day to visit Secombe again, and made my first offer: $2000 less than I was prepared to go, and $2000 less than he was prepared to accept. I dismissed the "other buyer" from my mind; he wasn't really in the running. If he *had* been, he would have bought the house by this time, wouldn't he? Secombe said he'd think about it.

That evening I telephoned Secombe. "Well?" I said. He told me slowly that he thought my bid was a bit too low. He granted that the house wasn't new; but on the other hand, it was more than usually well-built. He had built it himself, and he had built it slowly and carefully. I could ask anyone in the neighbourhood, anyone in Fredericton, for that matter.

I decided to play for time. I told him that I'd have to think the matter over. I told him that he was asking a bit more than I really wanted to pay, for *that kind* of property. The implication was, of course, that I had plenty of money to spend—if and when I chose. And I told him that of course

I couldn't expect him to hold the property for my decision, so if the other fellow came through with the cash offer, well, I guessed he'd better accept it and I'd just be out of luck. I guessed I'd just have to take my chances. He thanked me for calling, and I imagined the discussion he had with his podgy little wife when he hung up the telephone. All right, I thought. I've got you.

The next day I waited until late in the afternoon and then I telephoned him again. I raised the offer I had made and moreover (this is important), I *doubled* the amount of down payment I would offer if he would hold the mortgage himself. I pointed out that the sale would be a good investment (I carefully used the term "investment") for him. He said that, well, he was tired of waiting. Wanted to get to Florida and get settled in. If I would meet him at his lawyer's the next morning, we would draw up the necessary documents and sign them. I said that that sounded like a good idea to me.

I went out immediately and, by way of celebration, purchased a Samson-Dominion automatic percolator at the Canadian Tire store—an automatic percolator is an excellent item with which to begin a new life in a new house. Back in my room that evening I prepared myself an entire pot of Maxwell House coffee, poured in two shots of Tia Maria (when I had poured the coffee into a proper china coffee-pot), and topped off each cup with a generous helping of whipped cream—which I whipped up in the glass provided by the Windsor Hotel. I had him. As we used to say when we shuffled and joshed one another while we stood outside the doors of the high school: I had him by the short hairs. I thought I had discovered that making money is an easy business if you have just a bit of savings behind you. For just a moment or two I toyed with the idea of going into the real estate business. But I dropped the idea after some second thoughts. First, it would bore me; second, I did not have sufficient capital for anything extensive; and third, any such venture would defeat the purpose of this one: to prepare myself for death, to take off my tie, open my collar, forsake my occupation as itinerant teacher, and do nothing but loll back and stare at the sky and the trees and admire the long brown legs and long brown hair of the maidens who walked by in such loveliness. With a cup of coffee beside me, a bar of Baker's Semi-Sweet chocolate, a McIntosh apple, and a large slice of cheddar cheese — everything looked very promising indeed.

We met at the lawyer's the next morning and signed the papers. I maintained a properly sober decorum throughout. "Have you got any family?" asked Secombe. "No," I said.

"You're planning to take in students?" (This is the usual way of financing one's house in Fredericton, which is of course a university town.)

"No," I said. "I think I'll just rent out the other side."

"The tenants there don't have a lease," he said. He'd told me that before.

After the papers were signed, Secombe assured me he'd be out by the end of the month. He and his wife had bought a mobile home stationed down in Florida. Would I like to buy any of the furniture or perhaps the lawnmower? I told him I'd give him ten dollars for the lawnmower, but no, I didn't want any of the furniture.

I offered too much for the lawnmower, which doesn't work very well at all. But not really. I was buying goodwill. After all, he was holding the mortgage. Still does, for that matter.

James Secombe and his wife moved out without any great fuss. On the appointed date I walked by late in the evening, concealed in the dusk. The moving van from the storage company was backed up to the door of their half of the duplex and the furniture was being loaded for storage, as if they expected to live forever. Old Secombe was taking down the venetian blinds and arguing with his wife. I could hear him protesting that *he* didn't want the fool things—what were they going to *do* with them? But she insisted; they weren't going to leave *any*thing.

When the blinds were removed, I could see into the rooms; there were great shadows on the walls where the furniture had been, and the ceilings were thinly painted. There was litter and bits of newspaper around the front steps, and a pile of old rugs used for packing. The house was empty as a skull; grotesque— like a skull with a candle in it.

The tenants were coming over with beer bottles in their hands to say goodbye and pay their respects. I suspected that they hated the Secombes. The tenants were both short, square-shaped little people. He was bald and brawny, and looked like an ex-wrestler. She was hard and worn like an old doll. Her face had once been pretty—that was clear enough—but it had gone tough. They offered beers to the Secombes (Mrs. Secombe refused, and the tenants downed two in short succession), and the four of them stood on the porch, gathered under the yellow light. They were all short except James Secombe, who had to bend down to hear them. They talked quietly, as if they were searching for something to say, making up conversation because they had to. In fact, what the tenants were probably trying to ascertain with their beers was this: what sort of fellow was I? Would I allow them to stay? They wished they had a lease. Secombe was shaking his head slowly. He didn't know. I slipped away and went back to my room.

As I had arranged, I met Secombe the next morning at the house. He was tired. I asked him if they had been moving out all night, and he agreed that they pretty well had. He gave me the key, and I unlocked my door for the first time.

He followed me in. He apologized for the fact that he and his wife, Sarah, had not had time to clean the place properly. That was all right, I said. He said that a little paint would put it right, and reminded me (out of the blue) that the tenants had no lease. He'd always been satisfied with the Garretts, he said. Did I want him to show me around, perhaps explain some of the peculiarities? All houses have peculiarities, he said. No, not right then, I told him. Then I tried the key in the lock several times. The bolt rolled out smoothly. Secombe was a man who kept his locks oiled.

It's a good house, he told me again. He'd built it himself and it had been well looked after. It was true. Secombe was a bit of a fool, but he was quite right: he was a good builder. The corners were still square after nearly thirty winters. There were very few cracks in the plaster-and-lath walls. They were real plaster-and-lath, he assured me. It was obvious. No wallboard.

He was becoming a bit sentimental about the house, and understandably so. He'd built it with his own hands. To him, I was nothing but money, and I intended to remain so. I found myself telling him how happy he'd be in Florida. Today it was a fine autumn day, but it was not difficult to imagine what it would be like in February, when the snow was up nearly to the level of the windows. The snow would be full of sand, old candy-wrappers, and dog-droppings. It would have a dirty black crust on it when the weather was bleak, grey, and gloomy. I envied him, I told him, having weather like this (I gestured) all the time. The sky was clear and without depth; the sun was golden. The trees were just beginning to turn. Would I retire to Florida in about twenty-five years? Never. Was I from around here? I ignored the question.

Well, he said, he sure did plan to enjoy the winters in Florida. Do a good deal of fishing, he figured. He and Sarah, now, they'd liked the house, but it was too big for them. They'd figured on having more children—their first had died—but they didn't, one way and another. He left it at that and then asked me if I was planning to get married. He did *not* say: "Young fellow like you."

No, I said. I added "not yet" so that he would not feel

silly for having asked the question. We shook hands and he got into his old blue Falcon station-wagon and drove off to meet the pudgy-faced Sarah, wherever she was.

I went back into the house and stood in the bare living-room, listening for sounds of the Garretts. There were none, and therefore I assumed that they had no children. But then, upon second thought, I realized that "out there", school had started. Perhaps their children were of school age. In that case they would have gone off to school.

I had become a property-owner. I actually *owned* all of that mysterious heating apparatus. The house has a hot-water heating system: big, hard, fat-rumped, old-fashioned radiators which smell like old teakettles when they come on; sometimes the pipes bang and rattle. The basement runs the length of the house, and it was only slightly damp. No sign of leaks anywhere, no tell-tale stains of old puddles. My half of the basement was divided from the Garretts' by a floor-to-ceiling wooden grill made of cheap, unpainted, rough wood. All of these empty rooms were mine.

I walked around in wonder. It was my home on the edge of the world, right on the edge of nothingness. More, it was my establishment: 696 Rodman Street, Fredericton, New Brunswick.

When I walked out into the morning it felt strange, and at first I thought it was because after all these years I had become an *owner*. Then I realized what it really was, and I almost laughed right out loud there on Regent Street. It was this: school had begun, and for the first time in my life I was not in the classroom. I was neither pupil nor schoolmaster.

I was in the real everyday world, and I was surprised to discover how quiet it was. How many of us realize that each day begins with a great deal of hustle and bustle as people rush to work and to school? How few of us know — we aristocrats, loafers, well-to-do, and ne'er-do-wells — how quiet everything becomes under the high sun of 10 a.m.

Mothers appeared with their toddlers. Mothers and wives were going downtown to shop where, miraculously, none of the shops were over-crowded! It was such an immense relief that it threw me off-balance.

I was walking — was taking a *very* long walk because I was going over the bridge and across the river to a fellow who dealt in second-hand furniture. I was walking because I had the luxury of time at my disposal. There was no necessity of taking a taxi-cab, or even the bus. Indeed, I walked for three or four hours that morning — all the way over to Bleeker's Second-Hand Furniture — and surely Bleeker was surprised to see me *walk* away (he would deliver, of course) after making my purchases. I neither asked him to let me phone for a taxi nor inquired about the frequency of buses. The very absence of my questions surprised Bleeker, and I was pleased with his surprise.

Bleeker is a strange, crippled fellow who operates a used-furniture store out of an abandoned filling-station. In front of the station there remains the weathered, and futile, sign: THIS STATION FOR LEASE. The plate-glass windows have been replaced by more durable plywood substitutes, of course, and the gas pumps have long since been ripped out. Bleeker's is the place you go for a bargain.

And surely you will get one, because Bleeker's ignorance and your knowledge do not conflict. This is not to say that he is not shrewd. He is. He has a room full of incredibly ugly used furniture which he sells at exorbitant prices to the poor people who stumble in there, desperate in their dreams. He sells them worn-out kitchen sets with chrome legs and chair-seats covered in cheap (and often ripped) vinyl. Both table and chairs wobble. And horrible pole-lamps. Stuffed hideous sofas, mangy and springy. The poor people buy these because they have seen them in their dreams in Simpsons-Sears, Eaton's, Zeller's, the K-Mart,

Metropolitan Stores. They cannot quite afford them. Bleeker warily realizes their dreams, and prices his goods accordingly.

What Bleeker does not know is that he has furniture of real worth in the middle of all that junk. And after I had cautiously circled around an aqua sofa (and priced it), I told him that I would settle for the spool-frame settee which was tossed atop a kitchen set in one corner of the littered room. To make him feel good, and because I would be returning, I told him I'd probably paint it up to make it look good. In fact, what I did was strip it down and give it a good soaking in a mixture of turpentine and boiled linseed oil. I replaced the rope webbing in it; I purchased foam-rubber pads at the K-Mart and had them covered with a dark burlap. It is a beautiful piece of furniture. I prize it highly, and whenever I look at it, I'm proud of it.

Bleeker provided me with the necessities for my home at a very reasonable price, thought he had done well, and agreed to deliver the goods the next morning.

I walked back to Queen Street, ordered some cheap white paint (both enamel and latex-base) from Simpsons-Sears, and carried one gallon of the flat white paint home with me. My legs were aching by the time I finally returned, and I was nearly exhausted by the time I unlocked the door of my house. But I was triumphant—a good day's business had been done—and once inside, I permitted myself the luxury of laughing.

Not for long, of course. I bought some brown bread, ready-cooked beans, and some apples from the Stop Shoppe, and set to work. By the next afternoon (I slept on the floor, in a sleeping-bag which I purchased for the occasion, and which may yet come in handy another time) I had nearly completed the downstairs. I covered Mrs. Secombe's hideous decisions of green, blue, and ochre. The dining-room was somewhat disheartening as a faint Secombe-blue *would* seem to fade through my pure, austere white, giving it the look of skim milk.

Late in the afternoon, at least four hours later than he had promised, Bleeker arrived with the furniture. One must become accustomed to things like that. And of course he expected me to help him unload his van, which I was pleased to do, of course. Because it was raining lightly, he had brought along old dry-cleaner's bags to cover the furniture with as we carried it in.

There was no real reason for that, of course. It just shows you his ignorance of values—and the very goods he sold. I had chosen my furniture carefully. It is furniture which will last, and certainly it would not have been affected by a few stray drops of rain, although I would not have expected Bleeker to understand that. I had purchased several tables—dining-room table, bedside table, kitchen table, end-tables—two old Morris chairs, a bed, and this large, sturdy old table which serves as a desk. All of this in addition to the prized settee, which was the first piece of furniture that I refinished. All were solid; all were wood.

And, you see, there's the trick. Buy wood. Wooden joints can be glued, can be wrapped with rags and glued, can be swollen. You can always make them tight. And the finish or even the quality of the wood makes little real difference. You take off the paint or the cheap commercial finish with Harmony House Paint Remover and rub the piece with steel wool. Then you stain it, oil it, or wax it. Even cheap wood—even *pine*—will begin to glow with its essential, *natural* good health.

Bleeker and I stacked all the furniture on the glassed-in verandah, and agreed that it was a good afternoon's job. He commented that it was a nice place I had here. Was I renting it? No, I had purchased it. Well, it was a good house. He stood around and I wondered if a tip was customary, but I didn't know and finally decided that it was better to be thought a cheapskate than commit a gaucherie, so we ambled through an aimless conversation. Perhaps he simply did not wish to go back to work. After a while he shook my hand and hobbled out to the old van. It has a crazy home-made sign on the door: BLEEKER'S, written in odd-sized letters, which drip.

When the superintendent of schools received my letter of resignation, written and mailed from Fredericton, he was undoubtedly surprised. At first, I'm sure, he tried to place me, because I am quite sure that he didn't know my name. Mind you, I was under his employ for only two years, but still you would have thought that he would have known who I was. But on his infrequent visits to the school building where I held forth he had come across me in the hallway, and immediately found it necessary to turn to talk to J. P. Schneider, who passed for a "principal" at the school. No, I'm quite sure that he never bothered to learn my name; I was merely a faceless employee to him. This does not particularly annoy me because, on my part, I had gone rather out of my way to remain anonymous. It's a good idea, particularly if you want to avoid the nonsense of serving as a chaperone for school dances and/or taking tickets at one of their basketball games. The games are particularly boring. I never found any of them interesting in the least except for the girls who served as "yell-leaders", and they had an entrenched silliness which was impervious to wit. At any rate, our superintendent of schools, who always wore dark-brown suits which did not suit him at all, had a head which was precisely one size too small for his body. Never mind. When I wrote my resignation I deliberately addressed it: "Dear Sir".

Then the reply arrived. He wanted to express his regret—my teaching had always been satisfactory (by which he meant it was unexceptional), and he was sorry to lose me. I? Lost? He still hadn't really *placed* me, despite a phone call to Schneider. I can imagine him beaming as he talked to Schneider, saying, "At any rate, he won't be difficult to replace," and Schneider, also laughing because he must and because he was pleased to have an occasion when he wanted to, laughing with him. The superintendent went on to express, however, his disappointment with my manner of resignation. Indeed, he was "somewhat astonished". Did I realize that I was giving up an excellent retirement scheme (he had worked on it with the officials), not to mention a certain amount of seniority. Seniority? After two years? The man was either sarcastic or careless with words. And did I seriously think that I could live without working? I thought *seriously* about very little else. He ended by saying that of course he would be pleased to supply me with a recommendation (he did not say "excellent recommendation") if I should decide to return to the profession. He did not offer to hire me again himself. That was all right. I was hired through the newspaper; it was fitting that I left by letter.

An incident, just before my leaving:

A Mrs. Hudkins came into my room at about 4 p.m., by which time even the dawdlers had found something interesting to do and had left for the Lebanese hang-out across the street or were ambling along the muddy streets, annoying householders. I knew her by sight because she was the wife of the principal of "the other" school and she prepared potato-chip casseroles for the various "teachers' get-togethers" which are held, depressingly, at the start of each school year. I knew also that she worked as a social-worker, although I let her explain all this to me when she arrived. "Let me introduce myself. I'm Georgia Hudkins, and I'm a children's officer," etc., etc., etc. She settled herself into the chair by my desk. She was a square woman in a brown coat with a round face like a potato.

"Do you have a pupil named Darlene Houghton?" she inquired.

"Yes," I said. I refused to ask for further information.

"Well," said Mrs. Hudkins, "could you tell me something about her?"

I opened my little green record book, which I kept precisely and neatly and hated it for that. I looked up Miss Houghton. "She's been absent four times this term, and her work is unexceptional. I should say that she is a determinedly average pupil — without working at it, of course."

"You don't know anything about her?"

"No," I smiled. "I'm afraid I don't."

"Well," she said, settling herself with satisfaction, "that young lady is in for a surprise. Thank you."

And with that, she left. Without a word of explanation. Naturally I did not follow her to ask any questions, nor did I run down to Schneider's office to seek further information.

But the next day, when Schneider's pet girl knocked at my door with a note which indicated that Miss Houghton was to go to the principal's office immediately, I went along.

I told Miss Houghton that she was wanted by the "high muckety-mucks" (they all laughed at that, but they'll laugh at nearly anything), and I told the class to keep their noses in their books — I would be back almost precisely a minute *before* they expected me. They grinned at me and made a show of reading their books, which is about the best one can expect.

That afternoon Darlene was wearing a beige "twin set" sweater and cardigan. She had on a soft-brown skirt. The "twin set" was set off by a strand of imitation pearls. She had long brown hair, a pleasant and attractive face with a minimum of make-up, and long brown legs. She wore hose. It was only then that I realized that she was the only girl in the class to wear hose.

Mrs. Hudkins was in the office, sitting beside Schneider. They asked Darlene to sit down in front of the desk in the chair provided, and she did. Although Schneider looked at me as if to ask me to leave, I was looking out the window and he hadn't the courage to call me to attention and give me my dismissal orders. I leaned against the filing cabinet by the door as if I were a part of the conspiracy.

Mrs. Hudkins began with statements like "We realize you've had a difficult home situation." Were her parents still separated? Darlene nodded that they were.

Schneider was not looking at any of us.

But despite the extenuating circumstances which she would not go into, Mrs. Hudkins continued, "a situation has arisen which cannot be ignored."

Darlene said nothing. She did not even ask a question—merely smoothed her long hair with her hand.

"Do you know what I'm talking about?"

Darlene said nothing. Schneider dared not look at her.

"Well, Darlene," said Mrs. Hudkins. "We have information that you have been working as a prostitute, that you have been meeting men from the construction project and charging them a fee for the use of your body."

She *must* have worked out that speech beforehand. She *could not* have said "the use of your body" right out of her thick head.

"Do you deny it?"

Darlene said nothing. She simply looked at Mrs. Hudkins with a steady, pleasant interest.

Mrs. Hudkins went on to say that from now on she would be checking on Darlene, and that Darlene would have to observe a curfew. If she broke the conditions of this probation, she knew what would happen, didn't she?

Darlene nodded that she understood.

Mrs. Hudkins said, "That's all, Mr. Schneider," and Schneider said, "All right, Darlene, you can go back to your class," and Darlene went back and then Mrs. Hudkins left. I think that I was the only one who was shocked—not at what Darlene *did* or *had done* but at her acquiescence. Good

God! Right then I wanted to whisper into her ear urgently, "Scream, cry, deny everything. Accuse them of being in cahoots. Claim you're being framed, anything!" But Darlene accepted everything—accusation, conditions, and threat.

But she had gone back to the room.

Schneider said, "Well, she's got pretty legs, I suppose. But I never would have thought it."

Then he started to say, "How much do you suppose she char—" But he took in my glance and decided against it.

"Pardon?" I said.

"Never mind," he said. "Never mind."

It was her coolness which angered me.

There is a knock at the door, and it is my tenants, the Garretts, puzzled and faintly truculent like Pekingese. They look up at me expectantly, waiting for me to tell them what to do. Therefore I invite them in.

They introduce themselves. He's Bud; she's Dorah. How do you do, I say. We stand awkwardly in confrontation for a moment, and then I seem to remember my manners and apologize for the state things are in. "I'm just getting moved in," I explain. "But there's a bit of painting which really ought to be done first."

Bud Garrett says he knows just how it is and that he's willing to give me a hand if I need any help. He says that he has a strong back and a weak mind. I smile politely and decline the offer.

It is appropriate to offer them coffee, and so I do, although I apologize for the fact that I have nothing but instant coffee to give them. This is not entirely true, but I do not wish to bring out my new percolator and put it to use at this particular moment. Bud says: "Is there any other kind?"

I say that there must be some cups around here somewhere and Dorah immediately offers to run over to their place and fetch some cups from their kitchen. And she can make coffee in a jiffy, she adds. But no, no, I stave off her offers, and show them that my electric kettle is quite handy, and even as I show her I fill it and plug it in. I place it on the floor and we all stand around it in silence until the steam begins to rise.

Dorah snaps her fingers. "Cream!" she says. "I'll bet you don't have any cream!"

I resist the impulse to snap my fingers in return and say that by golly I'll bet that I don't. I say that I have some canned milk somewhere. But she says that it is no trouble at all for her to trot next door for some milk—"We don't use real cream, of course"—and anyway, she thinks that she had better look in on the children. She has left them in front of the TV. They are probably watching some *dreadful* program.

Smiling broadly, I agree. She is gone only a moment, and while she is gone Bud and I stare at the kettle in silence. When I see her returning I drag some of Bleeker's late chairs in off the verandah. Bud helps me carry in an old kitchen table which some poor soul had painted a lime-green. "What a pretty table," says Dorah when she arrives.

I serve the coffee and she pours in the milk out of the milk-box. I hate the fact that milk comes in boxes. There is only one thing worse: plastic bags. But one cannot escape. The manufacturers and producers have us in their clutches. There is no longer a choice, particularly in the matter of necessities, like milk. What the great stupid populace prefers, we shall all get, whether we like it or not. This is called democracy.

We sip our coffee. Dorah is pathetically trying to look proper. She is wearing ski-pants and a print blouse. Well, at least she does not have her hair in curlers. It is not surprising that we find very little to talk about.

"Is your side pretty warm in winter?" I ask.

"Oh, sure. Sure," says Bud.

"Now, Bud, you know it isn't."

"Well," he says. "It *can* be."

"How do you mean?" I ask.

"Well," explains Bud, "it's kind of like this. See, old Secombe didn't want to waste fuel, he said. Kept it kind of cool."

"Cool!" says Dorah. "The place was *freezing*. You see, what he'd do was this." (She has lit a cigarette and is looking around for an ashtray. I give her an empty paint-can.) "Mr. Secombe would come over and ask us if our side was warm enough. He'd say that *his* side was plenty warm, but what about *ours*?"

"That's what he'd do," says Bud.

"So of course Bud here would say that sure, we were all right. Sure we were!"

"I don't know why I never told him," says Bud.

"You mean that the heat is included in the rent?" I say.

Bud looks up, startled. "Sure," he says. "Didn't you know?"

I look faintly puzzled.

"The whole place is heated by one furnace," says Bud. "It pretty well *has* to be included in the rent."

"Oh," I say. "Well, maybe I'd better think about having *two* furnaces installed. That would be fairer, wouldn't it? In that way you'd pay only for the heat you actually used."

Bud is pleased. "Yes," he says. "That would be fairer."

I do not believe that they realize that I am setting them up. And I wonder if I am — consciously. It is simply that I have already played out this scene so many times in my mind that I know exactly how it is going to go.

"Secombe was a tough landlord," Dorah blurts out. "He was always at me for one thing or another."

"He wasn't so bad, Dorah. We've lived worse places."

"Isn't *that* the truth! But he was always complaining about the children."

"How many do you have?"

"Three," she says. "Two boys—ten and five, and a girl, eleven. They're just kids. Normal kids, you know. They'd get to playing and forget they weren't supposed to get over into Secombe's side of the yard."

"Yeah," says Bud. "Secombe should have put up a fence. How do you expect kids to stay on one side of an imaginary line?"

"It's pretty difficult—I should imagine."

"Do you have any children?" asks Dorah.

"I hope not. I'm not married."

She blushes and laughs, then pulls a face at her husband. "Well, I had to find *out*, didn't I?"

"It's a big house for a single man," says Bud.

"Well, I like the comfort of space," I tell him. And then, swinging right out of that statement to catch them off guard (it's a trick I've learned), I say: "I suppose you'd like to know about your rent. I understand there's no lease."

Bud—what is he—the driver of a delivery van?—looks stunned. He's never played in this league before. I've caught him over a cup of coffee in a bare kitchen full of paint fumes. Dorah is dead silent.

"Yes," he says. "I guess we'd better know."

"Well," I say, kind of looking out the window, "I'm afraid it will have to be $200 a month. That might go down when I get the new heating installed."

"Wheeeew," he says slowly. "That's pretty steep."

"I know it is," I admit. "And I'm sorry. But I'm caught, you see." (I turn to them and give them a helpless gesture.) "Old Secombe holds the mortgage—and I had to make a whopping big down payment. I've *got* to have that much to meet the mortgage. And I'm afraid that $200 a month is pretty well the going rate for a four-bedroom house in this part of town."

They are silent—like children who have been admonished by the stern but fair teacher. They do not think to argue that the house is old and probably needs repairs.

Both arguments are valid, and if they had given them, I would have had to acknowledge them. But the sheer number of 200 was too much for them. Had I said 195, they might have thought they could swing it.

Bud's anger is beginning to show in the red lines under his eyes. "Well," he says, "at least we've already paid this month's rent."

"Sure," I say. "Sure. And what the hell, think on it for a bit. If you're looking around maybe we can work something out while you're looking. I can absorb a little."

They left, broken-hearted. It was probably a glum evening for them. And if they had known that I did not have a job, that I intended to live off the earnings of my duplex—why, there's no telling what might have happened. Bud might well have taken his fists to me.

And of course the $200 rent was not necessary to meet the mortgage. $100 would have done that nicely. I intended to live off the other $100.

At the end of the week Bud came over and told me that they'd be moving. He'd found a place on the other side of the river (less desirable). He was sad and I was sad with him.

But it was clear the direction that all the discussion with Dorah had taken. He said to me: "That Secombe is a son of a bitch, isn't he?"

"I believe you're right," I said. "I believe you're right. The plumbing is going to have to be replaced."

That, I'm afraid, was an out-and-out lie.

Two

I did not attempt to make my drapes myself. To have done so would have been as futile as it would have been foolish. Instead, I answered an advertisement in the Fredericton *Daily Gleaner*, and hired a Mrs. A. P. Merton—"Drapes & Slip-covers Made"—to do the job for me. I telephoned her and asked if she would be willing, and able, to do the drapes for a seven-room house. I made it clear to her that I was asking as a private individual, and not as the representative of a firm which was furnishing and decorating a "model home". Perhaps she knew of my house: 696 Rodman Street, a duplex. She said that she did not, and that rather pleased me. I value my anonymity.

But would she, I wondered, be willing to bring her sewing machine over here and do the work here? It would be much simpler, I pointed out — the house wasn't crowded because I had only just moved in, and I was quite willing to pay for a taxi. She said that was a bit unusual, but she would do it. We could set a price when she got here and judged the size of the job. If I decided not to have her do the work, would I pay for the taxi to return her and her machine to her home? Of course.

Mrs. Merton arrived. She was much as I expected her to be: a large, bulky person with shrewd and capable eyes. She walked slowly around the house and thought for a few moments. Then she named a price which seemed reasonable to me, I agreed, and she asked if she might use the lime-green table as a work-table. That was certainly all right with me. I showed her a swatch of the material I had chosen for the living-room and dining-room, and said that I would buy what was necessary. She had only to tell me. She said she would, and said she would like to make one condition.

What was that?

Would I please not stay in the house while she was working. She liked to work by herself. She would prefer to work while I was at work.

"I'm afraid that I'm retired."

She looked at me shrewdly. Was I, perhaps, the fellow who taught in the local high school last winter. No? She must have me confused with somebody else, she said. I replied that she was a perceptive judge of occupations, however. I had been a schoolteacher. "I thought so," she said.

Who was the fellow for whom she had mistaken me?

Oh, she didn't know his name. At any rate, I wouldn't know him.

Why had he quit?

She didn't know.

I suggested that perhaps he was simply bored with his job.

Mrs. Merton replied that he might well have been — but that was no reason to quit. She expected to be bored by *this* job, she said. Then she told me that the blue velvet material I'd chosen for the drapes for the living-room and dining-room was going to be the very devil to work with. Well, I said, I'd always *wanted* to have dark blue velvet drapes.

"Hmph," she said.

Then she said that she was ready to go to work right then if that was all right with me, and she gave me a look as if to ask if I were going to comply with her request to leave her in peace. I did so.

Consequently, for the next week I rose early (I was sleeping in my sleeping-bag on the bed I had bought from Bleeker), breakfasted on an apple and Instant Breakfast — I prefer the chocolate flavour — and went downtown just as soon as Mrs. Merton arrived. For three or four days I simply wandered in and out of stores — went down Queen Street and back up King Street — and indeed, I was in the stores so often that I began to worry for fear they would suspect me of being a professional shop-lifter. Already, when I went into Zeller's — I suppose it's the largest store in downtown Fredericton — the shop-girls greeted me with a look of recognition, and a second look which clearly typed me: "He's *just looking*; won't buy anything." And I *did* get to know the business section of Queen Street rather well: the Paradise Gardens restaurant (morning coffee), Gaiety Theatre, Gaiety Men's Shop, Richards Jewelry, Dalmy's (the most exclusive women's shop), across Carleton Street, Curll's (another ladies' shop), Fleming's English Wear, Metropolitan Stores, Woolworth's, Hall's Book Store, Van Dine's Shoes, Ross Drugs, across York Street with its scramble lights, the Victorian city hall on the other side, Neill's Hardware and Sporting Goods, Medjuck's

Furniture, Simpsons-Sears, George's, Levine's, and Herby's. I suppose that one could say that this was the very heart of Fredericton.

It was at Herby's that I made what I suppose was my first frivolous purchase in Fredericton. Herby's is a music store. That is, it sells records and musical instruments. But Herby's also has a coffee-bar which offers what is reputed to be the best coffee in town (I did not particularly agree with that evaluation) and, as well, an excellent, *huge* hot dog. Habitually I tried to arrive at Herby's just after lunch-time (when the crowd would be gone) or at about 4 p.m. Sometimes I was there at both times.

I was eating a hot dog with relish and mustard when I heard this song which a youngster was playing— probably listening to the record on the pretence of buying it. Finishing my hot dog and my coffee I inquired of a clerk about the song. That was a rather pleasant tune, I said. "Why," he said, as if surprised that I did not know, "that's Anne Murray."

"Anne Murray?" I said.

He had divined that I was something of a stranger, and explained to me that Anne Murray had gone to the University of New Brunswick, "up the hill", and that she had graduated in 1966. Clearly he was pleased by my independent assessment of her talents. I agreed that she seemed to have a unique timbre to her alto voice.

He looked at me carefully. Was I mocking him? He decided I wasn't. "Would you like to hear one of her records?"

"Please," I said. And he played the LP *What About Me.*

"You're becoming a regular customer," he began, and immediately I bought the record.

Then, of course, having bought the record, I had to buy a phonograph to play it.

I went into Simpsons-Sears and asked for an inexpensive record-player. "Do you want stereo or mono?" I was asked.

I looked at the record. "I'm afraid I'll have to have stereo."

He began to show me his line but I interrupted him. "What's the cheapest you have?" I asked, because I was already beginning to feel panicked. I couldn't afford a phonograph on the budget I had set for myself, and ridiculously, I began to blame Mrs. Merton for pushing me out of the house and into this.

The cheapest he had was $66.45. It was a portable phonograph with two four-inch speakers, he began to explain, but I said, "Will you take a cheque?" He examined my attire to ascertain my worthiness and found me sufficient. "Of course," he said.

Then I had to walk all the way back to Rodman Street carrying that "portable" phonograph because, if you think I was going to waste 50¢ on a taxi after my bout of extravagance, you are quite mistaken. Perhaps my budget could have afforded it; my conscience assuredly would not.

When I entered the house I found Mrs. Merton sitting on a stool in the bare living-room. "I've been done for an hour," she announced.

I said that the drapes looked very nice—they were exactly what I wanted.

"You'd better inspect the whole job," she said, and conducted me on a tour of the entire house, pointing out the pleating she had done, the troubles she had had, and how she overcame them. When I tried to assure her that I was sure she had done an excellent job she said that she wanted to *show* me. She had no intention of taking money for an unsatisfactory job, and furthermore, she had no intention of lugging all her stuff back over here to re-do *anything.*

When we had completed the tour, I insisted that I was satisfied, and asked her how she wanted to be paid—cheque or cash.

"Cash," she said.

"I really am quite impressed with the job," I said, and tried to urge a bonus on her. She refused it, flatly. "I just did the job I said I'd do." Would I telephone a taxi for her?

The taxi arrived and I helped her load her machine into the back seat, and then helped her in alongside it. "Thank you once again, Mrs. Merton," I said, but she was already talking to the driver: "Let's stop at the government store on the way back."

"*Thank* you," I said again.

She turned to stare at me and nodded her acknowledgement.

That evening I began to prepare for my "early retirement", which is to say that I began to prepare for my life's work.

I plugged in my *extravagant* phonograph (one does not *need* music to survive), and with the unique voice of the talented young Miss Murray in the background, I began to shove my furniture into place.

I tried to do it properly, of course — without rushing, because I have noticed that when people do things "for the time being" (whether it is moving into a house or approving of some idiotic legislation) the effect is that the temporary measure becomes, in time, the permanent one. I am reminded of all those "temporary" buildings erected during the Second World War.

I filled the closets first, and when they were full, I threw away all of the extra coat-hangers which the Secombes had surprisingly left behind. That was because I hate the sound of empty coat-hangers jangling against one another. That sound shatters my nerves as, I suppose, the scratching of fingernails on a blackboard upsets some people. That sound, however, has never particularly bothered me. I remember that I used to do that sometimes — just to annoy my pupils — and when I turned to look at them shivering and groaning and even squealing, I was surprised to discover that they were *enjoying* their discomfort. That's something to remember.

With Miss Murray singing to me — "What About Me"

and "Both Sides Now" were my favourites, and I began to look forward to them — I moved the heavy table into one of the upstairs bedrooms which was to serve as my study. With some difficulty I wrestled the walnut dresser which Bleeker had thought so little of into my bedroom. I attached its mirror to it. The mirror is so old that it has flecks in it. I rubbed the wood of the old dresser with polish, and sniffed at its salty walnut smell. I usually like the smell of old wood. It sometimes smells of old houses. On the other hand, sometimes it smells of old people, and that can be frightening.

I put the "extra" bed into the "spare" bedroom only for the sake of decency and decoration. For the fun of it, I did not put any slats in it. I was not expecting guests.

When my house was in order I looked at it objectively. All the walls were an austere white. The banister on the stairway was a shiny, antique black. The dark blue carpet on the floor matched the work of Mrs. Merton.

It was good. I had to fight down a feeling of exultation — the one you have when finally things are the way you have always wanted them.

I stood there in the living-room and listened to Anne Murray, who seemed to be bringing all my lost life back to me, and I began to sing along with her: "The Last Thing on My Mind".

The words got to me. Somehow or other they seemed to lift a corner of my consciousness, and before I knew it I was standing in the centre of my perfected living-room and singing along with Anne Murray on the chorus:

"I could have loved you better,
Didn't mean to be unkind.
Don't you know that was the last thing on my mind."

I was tired, of course. I had been under a certain amount of strain, trying to settle into a new house — into a new life, in fact, trying to prepare for that very difficult future which is only the distance between the present and one's death, and Anne Murray's voice was touching me—the lesson "too late for learning"; the lesson which was "made of sand". Nobody knows that like an ex-schoolmaster.

I was looking at the jacket of the record, at Anne Murray's feathery, ash-blonde hair, and that teasing, conspiratorial smile, when suddenly the phonograph went dead.

I checked the plug. No, a lamp worked in it. It must be the phonograph.

And at that moment I had to hold myself in. I wanted to kick in both four-inch speakers and smash the treacherous apparatus with my feet.

I felt a distinct feeling of betrayal.

I composed this advertisement:

> FOR RENT: Four-bedroom duplex. Near schools and university. Reply to Box____.

I took the ad down to the old *Gleaner* building (Victoriana still in decaying use, across from—and a match for—the pseudo-gothic tumble of the city hall), paid to have it run for three days, and returned home to wait for replies. I looked forward to them; wanted to *read* them. Conversations are no good; you can't control them. Telephone conversations are by far the worst. One is always off guard. The caller, being prepared, always has the advantage.

MY WORK: THE ALIEN'S GUIDE TO SURVIVAL

Before it is possible to think seriously of anything else, one must admit that democracy, while a noble and idealistic concept of governing ungovernable man, is essentially an unworkable *idea*, and has, in fact, never existed in practice to any great extent.

It is, in fact, a theory which has never been put to use because it is essentially *unnatural*.

If one is to survive, one must first of all admit this.

The essential error of democracy is the belief (it is in fact a hope, a wish) that all men are of equal worth. However absurd this may be, it is none the less understandable in terms of history. The fact is that Luther, rebelling against the egotism of the Roman Catholic Church (embodied in its Pope), put forth the view (quite an understandable, perhaps even a just one) that all souls are of equal worth. One will not argue with that—particularly if one is concerned with the state of one's soul and happens to have some belief (or hope) in a Hereafter. But this belief that all men's souls are of equal worth in the eyes of God (and perhaps they are; I am not denying that) soon became corrupted to the belief that all men are equally *perceptive*. This belief was put into practice by the *Congregationalists*, who decided that the church, and its offices, ought to be open to some sort of common selective practice. In no time at all (geologically speaking, or even historically speaking), the practice of a self-governing church came to be an *ideal in itself*. This gave rise to the idea of democracy, in which a soul's *worth* became confused with the hope that all men were *equally capable of understanding the workings of the world*, and indeed, of *governing*.

In short, the equal worth of one's soul became confused with the idea of an equal distribution of brains.

Any schoolmaster will tell you that brains are distributed unequally—and that the *just* do not necessarily receive the most.

And the idea of democracy, wherever it has been tried (I am thinking of course of the United States), has in the course of time been found wanting. It was inept as well as inaccurate to say that "All men are created equal."

And because human behaviour seems to be subject to laws analogous to those of physics or mathematics, any human society which has attempted to govern itself along the lines of this *ideal* has foundered upon the shoals of *natural law*. Water seeks its lowest level; the mass of human beings will select the representatives of the mass — that is, the lowest common denominator — to represent and/or govern it. Consequently it is not surprising that elective offices are filled with the most common and patent *fools*. We have come to have government of fools, by fools, and for fools. One need only consider the history of the United States to see this illustrated. Who could better represent the fallen state of man, better illustrate the essential stupidity of the masses, than Lyndon Johnson and Richard Nixon?

It is to be hoped that Canada will glance southward and take warning from this disaster, and . . . etc., etc.

Yes, I think that that will do very well as an outline — or at least as a beginning draft. With a little work I ought to be able to polish it into a good first chapter, with appropriate quotations and examples, of course.

However, it is unlikely that I shall find a publisher with any ease or rapidity. Mankind has never enjoyed being told a few "home truths", as it were. We much prefer to live in a world of illusion and delusion. (And yet delusion is a certain road to self-destruction; survival can take place *only* when one keeps one's eyes focussed on *reality*.)

But it has occurred to me that I might reach a wider, and more immediate, public if I simply incorporate my studies into various letters to the editors, and scatter these out across the continent — rather like planting seeds which, when they have grown and sprouted more seeds themselves, will eventually cover the continent. By that time, of course, the originator, the planter, will long since have been forgotten — but perhaps that's as it should be.

Of course, to make sure that my letters are printed in the various newspapers, I shall have to hang my philosophical discussions on various handy pegs. But this should not prove to be unduly difficult.

For example, my questioning of the intrinsic worth of democracy might well be incorporated into the reactions to more "newsworthy" discussions which attend upon industrial strikes.

Thus: "This union and every union bases its demands upon the premise that since all men are of equal worth, all men are deserving of equal pay. By their own logic they cannot stop until they have achieved the same amount of pay as the owner receives in profits. Then, of course, he will quit and go to work *for his own firm*, because it is easier and pays just as well."

And a few comments about how all this leads inevitably to a *welfare state* always go down well.

I shall work on it.

Tennie wrote the letter, of course. I can imagine that Corrie stood a little distance behind him, looking out the motel window, in fact, and she was probably pleased that the children had at last gone to sleep. She was almost certainly disgruntled at the amount of money they were having to spend on the motel, but on the other hand she was sure that everything would "come out all right", for the good and simple reason that everything always *had*.

The letter was headed by the letterhead, which of course served as a return address: "River Idyll Motel: Cabins and Cottages — Reasonable Prices". Tennie had neatly inked in the date under the slogan. But it was a mistake to use that stationery provided by the motel. I should never have done that myself, even if it meant buying more paper. The very address had a touch of panic to it.

But they were nearly desperate, and as I read the letter I thought to myself that they would almost certainly pay the rent I asked — and I knew this even before I read the letter. This was the letter:

Dear Sir:

This is in reply to your advertisement in the

Fredericton *Daily Gleaner*. To be frank, the residence described would seem to be exactly suited to our needs. I have just taken a position (Assistant Professor of English) at the University of New Brunswick. I have a wife and three children (two boys, ages five and seven, and a girl, ten), and I would be quite willing to sign a year's lease if the residence proves to be suitable. Although I am a newcomer to the community, I am sure that I can provide satisfactory credit and character references.

Yours sincerely,

Harrison T. Cord

I read the letter with interest—and, yes—with pleasure. The tone was exactly right. It seemed to hold in the eagerness which he undoubtedly felt at the news of my house—seemed to hold it in just enough to let me know that they would pay the top dollar, but, at the same time, indicating that they considered themselves to be of a slightly superior caste than any "landlord".

So my crude pleasure was made of the following ingredients: the fact that I, one-time secondary-school teacher (once, in desperation, a grade-school teacher), but now a man of leisure and property, would be renting part of my property to a university professor. I decided that Harrison T. Cord must have wrestled for a time with the temptation to put his academic initials after his name: B.A., M.A., Ph.D. I was pleased that he had desisted.

Smiling, therefore, I sat down to compose my own brief note of reply. It was simplicity itself.

Dear Professor Cord:

If you are still interested in renting my house, would you kindly drop by at approximately 4 p.m. on 22

September to view the premises. I would be pleased to meet you and your wife. Sincerely yours.

I signed it: "Possibly your landlord".

I deliberately made them wait a couple of days.

But at the appointed hour on the appointed day, Corrie and Tennie arrived. They arrived wearing blue jeans (both of them) and identical University of New Hampshire sweatshirts.

I was somewhat taken aback. I had resurrected my old blue suit, and had even considered sending it to the cleaners because it *smelled* of *chalk-dust*. However, I had contented myself with giving it a good airing and a harsh brushing.

These were to be my tenants.

They got out of their somewhat dirty red-and-cream Volkswagen bus and glanced quickly at the house. Corrie turned back to shush the children (who were in the back) and to offer them candy. Tennie looked at the house more carefully. Then, together, they went next door and knocked at the empty side of the house, at 698. That was perhaps inattentive or careless of them, because I had indicated my address quite clearly on the note I had written them. But on the other hand, perhaps it wasn't a mistake at all. Perhaps it was simply a way of looking in the bare windows while pretending to be making a mistake. I watched them leave that door and approach mine. It had rained the day before and there were puddles on the old sidewalk, but they walked carelessly right through them. Both were wearing thick white athletic socks and "loafers".

Then they knocked on my door, and I opened it. They greeted me with warm, hesitant smiles.

"Come in, come in," I said.

And they entered, ready to be pleased.

As soon as she saw my blue carpet, Corrie said quickly, "Here, let us take off our shoes before we track mud in."

I tried to dissuade her, but she would have none of it. As if to set an example, she took off her shoes, and then Tennie took off his.

"I'll put them on the porch," she said. But I said not to be silly, they would get cold out there. "Here," I said, and put them right inside the door.

"Don't you have a newspaper or something we could put them on?" asked Corrie.

"No, no," I said. "Never mind." She straightened the shoes, to make them neat, side by side: hers, small; his, large.

"Come on in the living-room and sit down," I said. "I have a pot of coffee all ready."

Corrie was dismayed. "The children . . . ?"

"They're all right in the bus," said her husband. "It's not cold."

I thought of offering them some hot chocolate for the children, but that would merely have confused matters. The children would just have to sit out the impatient time in the car — fighting with one another if they could find nothing else to do — until we had finished. I chided myself, however; I should have planned for them.

But I said: "Come on in, sit down," and I showed them into the living-room. Corrie walked in on the toes of her white-socked feet, like a dancer.

"We've been living rather hand-to-mouth," said Corrie, as if to explain their casual attire. Then she caught sight of my beautiful spool-frame settee. "Oh, what a beautiful sofa," she cried. I told her how I had found it over at Bleeker's and how I had refinished it. I explained that they (she and her husband) could probably furnish a house quite inexpensively by going to Bleeker's. Did they have much furniture?

"Only the barest essentials," she said. Her husband agreed that perhaps they ought to look into the possibility of getting some furniture from Bleeker.

"We didn't have much," she explained, "and we sold some of what we had. We didn't want to bring much across the border." She added that they were Americans.

I said: "I gathered that."

The mugs were ready on the tray in the kitchen. I poured them full of coffee, and placed a bowl of sugar and a bowl of whipped cream beside them. In the living-room I heard them talking in low tones about the children. Tennie suggested that perhaps she ought to go out and stay with the children while he talked to me, but Corrie was having none of that plan.

When I returned, Corrie was looking over my living-room with an intense interest. Then she turned her dark-brown eyes to me. "Your house is lovely," she said.

"Thank you," I said. "I enjoy my creature comforts."

"Yes," she said. And then: "Would you show us your house?"

I said that I would be pleased to, although I warned her that there wasn't much to see.

We started toward the stairs. Tennie seemed to hang back in the living-room, but then he seemed to have decided that he might as well tag along.

"Is the other side just like this?" asked Corrie as we climbed the stairs.

"Exactly," I said, "although it isn't fixed up much. Both places were rather dingy when I bought them. The other side needs painting." I added that if they wanted to paint it—if they took it—they could choose the colours and I would pay for the paint.

Behind me I noticed that Tennie, who is rather tall, was ironically checking the height of the doors with his head—standing up very straight and solemnly in the middle of the doorway and nodding his head. Of course his head did not bump. I presume that he was satisfied that the doors were of sufficient height. He remarked that it was very generous of me to offer to pay for the paint.

"Not at all," I replied. "Contented tenants are cheaper in the long run."

Corrie was excited by the "possibilities" of the upper hall, and there was no keeping her on a guided tour. She spied the cupboards and drawers set into the wall by the bathroom.

"Look at these cupboards!" she said. "We could have two drawers for each of the children." She pulled open the top drawer. It was empty.

"I haven't lived here very long myself," I explained.

Tennie was looking out the window of the corner "spare" bedroom and checking it by sliding it up and down. "Does it cost much to heat?" he asked.

I had to admit that I didn't know, and I repeated that I had only just bought the place and hadn't yet lived in it for a winter myself. I explained the furnace arrangements which had caused the Garretts such consternation—although I tried to indicate that I was more than willing to be liberal in these matters.

Corrie was like a child, set loose to "explore" in a new house. She called out from the other spare bedroom—"Tennie! Look at the size of the closets!" But Tennie had by this time moved into the bathroom, where he was turning the water on and off, listening for the rattle of pipes. They did not rattle. Secombe had been proud of that.

Having once read a book on "How To Buy a House", which recommended that one check the water-pipes for "rattle", I presumed that Tennie had read a similar book.

Corrie and Tennie met again in the hallway. "We can put the two boys in the back room, and Alisha can have her own, and you can use the little one for a study."

Tennie agreed that seemed to be a reasonable plan, if they took the house. He was trying to hold down Corrie's evident enthusiasm, but without much success.

When we came back downstairs I poured them fresh

cups of coffee. Tennie tried to demur, but Corrie said: "Oh, come on, we've got time for one more cup," and turning to me – "May I smoke?"

"Of course," I smiled, and fetched her an ashtray. She lit a cigarette gracefully, and looked around the room with bright eyes, as if she were already planning where she would put her furniture. I could almost see her reaching certain decisions – for example, that they would *have* to buy a table to go under the window.

"Do you have your own stove and refrigerator?" I asked. I did not particularly want to have to provide those items, although I would have done so if it had been necessary.

"As a matter of fact, we do," said Corrie, pleased with herself. "We were told to buy our appliances on the other side of the border before we moved up here, so we did. Luckily," she laughed, "we had a *little* money."

"And how do you like New Brunswick – thus far?" I asked.

"Hmmmm," she said, sipping at her coffee and pulling at her cigarette until its end glowed. "So far we like it very much indeed." Her lipstick had smeared the filter-tip of her cigarette. She put it on the ashtray. "You know, when we moved up here we had to drive up through Maine – we crossed the border at Calais – it *is* pronounced Callus, isn't it?" I nodded. "And it rained and rained and rained. And then, when we got to St. Stephen, the sun came out! It was lovely," she said. "Northern Maine seemed so desolate – as if we were running off the edge of the world, and then suddenly life seemed to begin again at St. Stephen. And the customs people were very nice to us."

Tennie said that moving to New Brunswick from the U.S. was no easy trick, and he began to tell a story which, it was plain, he had already told several times before – about how he had tried to hire a moving firm to move them to Fredericton, and how none of the moving firms seemed to know where New Brunswick was, for God's sake, and kept insisting that it was in New Jersey or even in Florida, and when he told them that it was north-east of Maine, they had argued vehemently that "Mister, there's *nothing* north-east of Maine."

Then Tennie set out on a brief lecture on the egocentricity of the United States of America. I interrupted to point out that American tourists were forever trying to use U.S. postage stamps when they came to Canada—"as if the border did not exist". Tennie supposed it was an easy error to make—because of the matching postal regulations and the ease of sending mail back and forth between the U.S. and Canada.

"Tennie," Corrie interrupted. "Can we afford it?"

"I don't know," he said, facing up to the problem at last. "You'd better ask the landlord about the rent."

"The rent is $200 a month," I said. "But that includes the heat—at least *this* year."

That was fine with Tennie. Did I want a lease?

No.

Did I want a month's rent in advance?

No, that wouldn't be necessary.

"You know we have three children," said Corrie suddenly.

"Yes," I said. "You indicated that in your reply to my advertisement." I pointed out that I had taught school for several years and as a consequence had no fear of children and even fewer illusions about them.

Corrie turned to Tennie. "Are we really going to take it?"

Tennie replied that it certainly looked that way. Corrie looked quite relieved. "Thank you," she said to her husband.

I had to point out to them that they hadn't actually seen the house itself, although it was exactly like this one, and I tried to urge them to go next door before they made up their minds. But Corrie didn't want to do that. With a comical shake of her long brown hair she said: "It's more fun this way. It gives us something to look forward to."

I said I hoped they wouldn't be disappointed (Corrie said that she was sure they wouldn't), and I gave them the key. They would move in the next day, she said. Their furniture was in a bonded warehouse out on the Vanier highway and a telephone call would have it here the next morning. Then Corrie thanked me very quietly and gently. "You have no idea how scruffy life has been these last couple of weeks," she said. "Thank you."

I said I was pleased to have rented the house so easily. I watched them put on their identical loafers to go with their identical sweatshirts. They left. I noticed, oddly, that Corrie had an extraordinarily beautiful collar-bone. It seemed to be emphasized by the stretched neck of the old sweatshirt. They got into their VW bus, which rocked under the excited agitation of the children, and drove away.

I have rented my house.

In my satisfaction, I recall certain incidents. For example, when I first started teaching (in a decidedly fourth-rate high school which did not possess so much as a school library and, worse, saw no reason why it needed one), I found it necessary to reprimand a scruffy boy. As I found out later, he was an inveterate trouble-maker, and within weeks after dropping out of school (my failing him for copying an article out of the Encyclopaedia Britannica was only one contributing factor among many), was in difficulty with the authorities. I told him as gently as I could that his work showed evidence of "lack of personal preparation". I believe that was the euphemism employed.

He looked up at me with utter scorn and said: "If you're so smart, why ain't you rich?" Merely asking that particular question confirmed him in the rightness of his own opinions.

It is now true, of course, that while I am not rich, I have

one of the advantages of being rich— perhaps the central one. I do not have to work.

Nor would that young boy's impertinent (and irrelevant) question have unsettled me at all if that had been the first time it was asked.

But when I was in the seventh grade I sat behind a girl named Kristen. She was quite tall (taller than I was at that time), and, I suppose, she embodied all that a boy would have thought of as beautiful. She had blonde hair and blue eyes. I sat at my desk, with its black, inked, ancient, scratched initials and crude drawings of a dog (like cave-drawings), and its dry, empty inkwell, staring at the graceful falling of her fine blonde hair. It had a gentle wave just above her collar.

She caught me quite unprepared. We had been required to write an essay on some topic or other, and as usual I had done the best I could and had recopied my work before I handed it in. When the teacher handed our papers back, Kristen took a quick look at her own, and then turned around suddenly and demanded to see mine. Silently I passed it forward to her. At the bottom was the teacher's inscription in fine red ink: "A + This is excellent work."

Kristen threw it back at me. "If you're so smart, why ain't you rich?" she said.

I no longer work for a living; I'm renting my house to a university professor. And I no longer give a snap for either of you!

On the day that Corrie and Tennie moved in I decided to be a little—well—"eccentric". It was not that I feared knowing my tenants, of course, but it is a good idea to cloak oneself in an aura of eccentricity. It gives one a certain freedom from *conventional expectation.*

Consequently I decided not to be at home on the day that they moved in. After all, they had their own key.

But I did leave them a little note — on a 3 x 5 card, in a white envelope — telling them about the procedures of garbage collection in Fredericton. I informed them that, in Fredericton, garbage was garbage, and it was not necessary to separate bottles from paper, nor paper from banana skins. Garbage collection is on Tuesday.

I can quite imagine Tennie's reaction when he opened the door and found the note there on the floor. He probably said, half to himself: "What a damn strange thing to do!"

And then, when Corrie ran next door, as she undoubtedly did, she found only a neatly typewritten note on my door: I'VE GONE OUT; I'LL BE BACK.

They probably had to buy light-bulbs at the Stop Shoppe. The Garretts, in their petty anger at being finessed out of their home, had stripped the house.

Although I have seen very little of Corrie and Tennie (and their family), circumstances have allowed me to know a great deal about them. For example, I know from the thumping on the stairs that they arise at 7 a.m., and other sounds indicate that Jack, the elder boy, is a slug-abed and difficult to wake. He has to be called two or three times before he will leave his snuggly covers. Then at 8 o'clock Jack and Alisha leave to go to the Montgomery Street School (which alone among Fredericton schools begins its day at 8.30), and at 8.45, Tennie leaves for the university. From this I deduce that he has his first class at 9.30. At 10 or so — she is unpredictable — Corrie comes out with Robert in tow — both of them bundled up in various coats, furs, and mittens, although winter is only just here and it is wise to delay wearing the heavy apparel until the last possible moment so that it will have its *maximum effect*. They go downtown.

Robert, of course, is a curious little fellow. He is just leaving his infancy for childhood, and consequently he is forever picking up discarded candy-wrappers, ice-cream sticks, and non-returnable bottles. He must *feel* them to know what they are, even before he has a name for them.

The university students who patronize the Stop Shoppe are responsible for the incredible litter which is observable for blocks around. It is to the credit of the Stop Shoppe that a litter bin has been provided, but the students ignore it with the lordly abandon of youth. I have spoken to the manager of the store about the iniquity of non-returnable bottles, and he agrees with me that they are a curse. He does not consider the alternative – that he refuse to sell "pop" at all – because, presumably, this is how he makes his living. Therefore he sells that of which he does not approve.

When Corrie and Robert go out in the morning, young mother and infant son, she seems to find it necessary to urge him to "hurry up", although in fact there is no reason whatever for haste. They have plenty of time to get back. Tennie does not come home for lunch, and Alisha and Jack are never back before twelve.

It is possible that, from time to time, Corrie telephoned me. I do not know because usually I do not answer my telephone. Indeed, in those first few days when they were the "new" tenants of my house, I saw relatively little of them – there was the merest (if cheery) "Hello" when she and I happened to meet on the street, or pass one another going in or out of the house. Indeed, her first communication with me was a brief note I found one morning in my mailbox.

It was on a Monday, I believe, because it said something like this: "Dear Landlord. Would you come over and join me and Robert for a mid-morning cup of coffee and a piece of apple pie on Friday morning? I make a delicious apple pie. Come over about 10.30. Love, Corrie Cord."

I thought that she used that word "love" rather lightly, but inasmuch as she had set the date sufficiently far into the future for me to reply by post, there was little I could do. I reflected that in fact I had been trapped by my own *postal devices.* There is no use protesting about that. Consequently, I wrote her a letter saying that I would be pleased to join her for coffee and apple pie. When I went out to post the letter at the mail-box in front of the Stop Shoppe, I discovered that Corrie was waving at me from her front window. When she wants to be, Corrie can be as sly as a cat.

When I arrived that morning, Corrie was wearing the same freshly laundered University of New Hampshire sweatshirt that she had been wearing when we had first met. This pleased me, and I was proud of the fact that I had foreseen the proprieties of the occasion and worn a dark blue pullover sweater and a new pair of corduroy slacks (Simpsons-Sears) myself.

It was clear that she had gone to some trouble to prepare for the occasion. The house was as neat as a pin, and she had already set out the coffee-pot, the cups and saucers, the plates, and the pie, waiting my arrival.

She poured the coffee, I looked around, and she explained. She and Tennie had decided not to paint after all. "There just wasn't time." So the house was still possessed of the Garretts' undistinguished light-brown walls. However, the pie, made from recently harvested McIntosh apples, was fresh out of the oven. Corrie's timing was perfect. As she cut the pie, Robert was clamouring for a piece for himself, and Corrie had to tell him that it was "hot—*too* hot". She glanced up at me with something like pride. Then Robert was suddenly aware of my presence, and became very silent, tucking himself behind Corrie's legs when she rose to serve me.

The pie naturally led me to tell Corrie about the Boyce Market (or the York County Market), which is usually referred to simply as "the market". "It's a farmers' market," I explained. "Every Saturday morning the local farmers bring in their produce to sell, and you can buy meat and vegetables and apples — particularly apples — of much higher quality, and much more cheaply than you can find at the supermarkets."

For a moment I believe that Corrie was slightly offended — as if I were indirectly criticizing her pie.

"Isn't the pie good?" she asked.

"Of course it is," I assured her. "The fact is that it is probably made of local apples." Then I got her to fetch the empty plastic bag they had come in, and sure enough, they were from a grower out in Keswick Ridge. "There," I said, "you see? However, you could probably have bought them more cheaply at the farmers' market."

She said that that was very good to know, and I, fearful that I had inadvertently insulted her, apologized for talking about money — particularly in such domestic terms. She assured me that that was quite all right, and she needed all the help she could get.

Because I wanted to put her at ease, and because (in a way) it is true, I told her that I was a glutton. An absolute glutton, I said. I insisted upon it. She urged more pie on me and I ate three pieces. It is true. I am passionately fond of apple pie.

By this time Robert had filled himself up with pie, and he made his way out from behind his mother's legs and sat at my feet. Then he stared at me with slow interest — and untied my shoe-laces.

I asked about the children. Well, explained Corrie, rosy-cheeked Alisha was the eldest and would probably be a beauty when she grew up. Jack was next and wanted to be a biologist. Lately he had been after his father to buy, or build, some cages so that he could keep animals in the basement. This was the first time they'd lived in a place with a decent basement. Would that be all right with me?

Of course it would, I assured her. What animals did they have in mind?

They were thinking in terms of a hamster—or perhaps a gerbil. Gerbils don't have any smell, she explained.

"No rats?" I teased her.

No, she did not like rats—or mice.

Well, I said, they could certainly keep animals in the basement. In fact, if they got a gerbil, I would like to see it. They could even keep a dog if they wished. I had no rules against children or pets.

That pleased her. She had always wanted to have a dog, although Tennie was not *at all* enthusiastic about the idea.

And what *about* Tennie, I asked. Was he happy with his post at the University of New Brunswick?

Corrie smiled lazily. Oh, yes, she said. He was happy enough. And he would be—for a while. She explained to me that Tennie was "ambitious". "He had his Ph.D. at the age of twenty-four," she said, "which is just a *little* early." But he would be content for a year or two if he found enough challenges to keep him busy, and just a little co-operation.

Robert was still concerning himself with my shoe-laces. Corrie directed her attention to him, watched him gnarl my laces into odd, individualistic little knots, and then picked him up and put him on her knee. She stuck her face into his and rubbed noses with him. "Shoe-laces and food," she teased him. "That's all you care about." He laughed, and squirmed to be put down.

I mentioned that perhaps I ought to be "getting back".

"To what?" she said, tactlessly.

I felt as if I had been "caught out" at something. And what was I to tell her? That I had to get back to my own private life? No, I was not going to tell her anything. Instead I asked her a question: "Why is your husband called 'Tennie'?"

"Oh," she laughed quickly, "that's because of his middle name."

"I'm afraid I don't quite understand. Is it a family name?"

"Nothing so simple as that," she said. She had to rush after Robert, who had nipped quickly into the kitchen and, from the sounds, was exploring the garbage bag. Corrie had to shout the conversation to me while she wrestled with Robert. "His middle name is Tennyson," she shouted. She came back into the living-room, wrestling with the recalcitrant Robert and laughing—perhaps at him, perhaps at the anecdote she was telling me. "After Alfred Lord Tennyson. Tennie's mother was a Romantic."

No sooner had she told me than I wished that she hadn't.

To cover my confusion I said, "Well, I have deduced, anyway, that you both went to the University of New Hampshire."

"What?"

"The sweatshirts," I explained.

Corrie began to laugh and almost tripped over Robert, who apparently thought it a good opportunity to try for an escape. She continued to laugh, and it became increasingly obvious to me that I had committed something of a *faux pas.*

Perhaps, I thought, they had been asked to leave the University of New Hampshire. Perhaps Tennie had been fired for unorthodox teaching methods—or experimenting with drugs. Perhaps he had instigated a student rebellion.

But before I could further embarrass myself, Corrie explained that neither she nor Tennie had ever even considered attending the University of New Hampshire. They had been driving through Durham, New Hampshire, and bought the sweatshirts as a joke. "It's kind of a family joke," she said. "I've never even been to college," she said, somewhat subdued.

Attempting now not to look at her sweatshirt, and laughing with her to cover my embarrassment, I said that now I really must be going.

"But wait," she said, as if she expected me to dart out

the door that moment. She gestured helplessly with her hands. "You know, . . . we haven't . . . we haven't paid our rent yet."

So that was the reason she had invited me over. She wanted to raise that particular matter. I could imagine them plotting the entire scheme and Tennie saying, "Well, although I hate to do it, I suppose we ought to pay the old fellow the rent sooner or later."

And for my part—I was thinking that probably they simply hadn't set up their accounts yet, or perhaps Tennie had not yet been paid and they were rather short right then. Or perhaps I actually expected them to send me a cheque through the mail.

Consequently, I tried to indicate that no explanations were necessary. I said that surely a few days' grace were in order. I realized that they were new in town, but I was sure that their credit rating was entirely satisfactory. In fact, I never did bother to check it.

But no, no, Corrie was laughing. I didn't understand. She was still laughing. She had a Bank of Montreal chequebook in her hand.

If she insisted, I said, she could write me a cheque. There was no hurry. I wouldn't get to the bank for a few days.

"But . . . " she said.

"But?"

She blushed. "But I don't know your name."

"Didn't Tennie tell you?"

"He didn't know it, either."

"But he wrote to me."

"He wrote to a box number."

"Well," I said—a bit exasperated, I'm afraid—"my name is William A. Boyd."

She bent over her chequebook (holding Robert clasped firmly between her knees) and began to write; then she looked up.

"Isn't that the name of the old cowboy star?" she said.

Well, whoopee. Little old Billy Boyd. How are you, son? Shyest boy in the block. Known as "Hopalong" to his distant uncles, each of whom thought that the joke was new with his perception of it, and each of whom produced a new white cowboy hat to go with it. I must have had four or five of the damned things hidden under my bed, and I never wore one once. Hopalong Cassidy, pale and pure as ice-cream, bland as tapioca, riding around the same Hollywood hill in every movie on the same white horse, doing in the baddies for the sake of the goodies. All puns intended. I went to see his films in the same way as a kid picks scabs on his knees. I did not pick at the scabs on my knees. When television resurrected Hopalong Cassidy from his Saturday afternoon graveyard, there was a resurgence of the joke. Once, on Faculty Night, I was given a white hat and a matched pair of Texan cap-guns.

"It seems to me," she mused, "that William Boyd was the real name of Hopalong Cassidy."

"I'm afraid I don't know," I said. His real name must be the worst-kept secret in the history of Hollywood.

But then she said: "Oh." She realized what she had done, and her mouth was open with pity for me and the inexplicable regret of having said something which could not be taken back.

"I'm sorry," she said. "I should have known. I, of all people, should have known. I should not have told you about Tennie's real name, either. I'm very, very sorry." I think that she was nearly ready to burst into tears.

"I somehow didn't think," she tried to explain. "I mean . . . this is a foreign country to me . . . I didn't think about Hopalong Cassidy."

"I'm not a Canadian," I said.

"You're not?"

"No," I said. "I'm an American."

"You're not!" she said. "You're not. I mean . . . " She blushed a deep red. It went right down her lovely neck.

"I'm sorry," she said. "I couldn't tell."

"There's nothing to be sorry about," I said, and I felt a warm glow of pleasure. What could be more delightful for an alien than proof that he is blending in with the native-born; proof that he has successfully become anonymous; proof that he has in fact *been born again in his chosen character in the country of his choice.*

Smiling with pleasure, she advanced the blue cheque to me as if it were a gift, a peace-offering.

And then I blurted out the fact that she and her husband were supporting me, that I was living off the income of the other half of my duplex, that they were my livelihood.

"Good God, we're not!" she said.

"I'm afraid you are," I said. I told her that I had no job and did not intend to get one. "You and Tennie are buying my freedom," I said.

She laughed and said that she thought that was lovely. It was a grand joke.

"But I don't want you to feel responsible," I said, foolishly.

"Responsible?"

"You're supporting me," I said.

Then I was rushing and shuffling, trying to get out the door, and wishing that that damned little Robert had not chosen that moment to be quiet and stare at me as if I were some interesting object. I was at the door, and Corrie was trying to say goodbye and calling after me, "Next time I'll try to have some whipping cream for your coffee."

"Don't do that," I said.

"Why not?" she called. "I like to keep things in my house for my friends."

"But it *won't keep*," I said.

Three

The American Thanksgiving has passed, virtually unnoticed except by Corrie, Tennie, and me. I was invited over for a taste of turkey with the children. After the children were put to bed, we sat in the living-room and discussed the scarcity of things to be thankful for. Tennie held forth (wittily) on the disastrous policies of all nations, and particularly on the errors of the United States of America. I cannot say that I disagree with him in any great detail, but he has an insufficient grasp of scope—of dimension. The result is that his lectures are facile and clever without being terribly intelligent. He *will* slant his discussion to make the small point, and quite ignore the larger.

For example, he will say, "Whether you agree with it or not, whether you participate in it or not, and no matter what side you are on, you cannot escape the fact that violence has taken over as the American way of life."

He is satisfied with this. My point is that man is a violent animal. My interests are supra-national.

The weather is already cold, surprising me. I had expected it, but am none the less surprised. A coldness is already settling into the ground; the dead grass is stiff with it. My furnace runs more often than I like to hear it. I have calculated that it costs me approximately 5-10¢ each time it turns itself on. It might easily turn itself on twenty times in a day, although I haven't yet kept an accurate count.

The cold is closer to you. You feel as if winter, or death, is reaching out for you.

AN ALIEN'S GUIDE TO SURVIVAL (Continued)

Within certain limitations, man is as he is by choice. But I must stress that reservation: "within limitations". A man has no choice about being born — or when or where he shall be born. (I suspect that most of us would choose other circumstances if we were but given the opportunity.) Nor has man a choice about the fact of death. By careful preparation a man may choose the place of his death, or, if he is willing to hurry matters a little, he can even choose the circumstances of his death — within the fairly tightly circumscribed limitations of the knife, gun, rope, or poison. But he *cannot choose not to die.*

Therefore it follows that man identifies himself and/or creates himself only within the time allotted between those two significant points. But within his limitations, man has a surprising latitude of decision. For example, he can choose to live in one country or another. He can choose to attempt one occupation or another. He can choose to create for himself a life which, he believes, suits him.

However, the choice is not made without risk, and therefore it requires *courage.* For example, a man may choose to live in West Germany rather than East Germany, or Cuba rather than the United States (or vice versa), but the choice in each case entails a certain amount of *risk*, and therefore requires a certain amount of *courage.*

Yet, I would recommend that one accept the alien's challenge, that one, for various *reasons*, become an emigrant/immigrant. The immigrant can choose to create for himself an entirely new life and consequently can choose to create himself as he wishes himself. (I do not deny that this is not *easy*: the immigrant is always suspected of betraying his native country, and is usually judged guilty of not having been *born* in his adopted one.) *However*, it is the great advantage of the immigrant that he is *free of his past*, that he is virtually born again in his new country. Indeed, it was Christ who stressed the necessity of *choice*, and offered something of a like reward: if you chose Christ you could be reborn *in Christ.* You would achieve the *new life.*

However, I must stress the fact that any sort of *move* associated with *choice* is not easy. For example, an immigrant from the United States to Canada comes always under the shadow of history—or, to be more specific, the shadow of Benedict Arnold. Arnold, who was considered to be a traitor to both King and Congress (an American easily forgets the first treachery), came to New Brunswick (Saint John) in 1785, and opened a general store and later did a bit of trading with the West Indies. However, when he was absent on a trip to England his store in Saint John burned to the ground, and it was alleged that he had ordered his son to set it to the torch, and had deliberately over-insured the property. When he brought suit for libel against his one-time partner, he was awarded the judgment—but received only twenty shillings in damages (and this indeed was larger than the sum desired by certain jurors, who wished to give him only sixpence). He later moved here, to Fredericton, but shortly went to England. (See *New Brunswick and Its People*, by Stewart MacNutt.)

I still owe over half the sum due on the stereo set, and am appalled by the ease with which I gave in to the touch of *luxury*. I enjoy Miss Murray's singing, but her presence in my home is not necessary. And the Simpsons-Sears bill also contains such items as one pair of corduroy trousers and a new blue sweater. It now looks very doubtful if I shall have a new furnace installed next spring. Because I do not believe that I ought to dip into my savings—which are a comfort behind me—I do not believe that I shall be able to complete certain non-essential innovations (a fence around my property to ensure privacy and protect it from the litter from the Stop Shoppe). The profits will not bear it. I must support myself first. If someone should ask me if I were willing to go to work for the sake of my house, I would say (now), "Never."

If the number of non-returnable bottles which seem to grow on my lawn each night were returnable, I should easily net $1 per day.

I meet Corrie in the basement these days. The fact is that when she goes down to the basement to do her laundry, I hear the sound and, because I do not recognize the rumbling of her washing machine at first, I think that perhaps there is something amiss down there—so I trot down. I come around my furnace and there, just on the other side of the floor-to-ceiling grill (it is made of a cheap, rough pine), is Corrie (and Robert). She has strung a little line across her half of the basement, evidently to hang her dainty and colourful underthings on, because she uses the dryer for her heavy laundry. Robert spies me and sets up a howl, and Corrie greets me in her cheery and slangy manner ("Hi, Bill") and we sometimes hold genial conversations in the most absurd of circumstances. I am on one side of this massive grill, like a tiny priest in a huge confessional box. Once she even held up one of her brassieres and said to me (mocking one of the more popular television commercials): "How's this, Bill? — Whiter than white?"

But usually we simply make "small talk". She asks me how the great philosophical treatise is coming along, and when I try to explain its essential concepts to her, she says she doesn't understand and suggests that perhaps we ought to talk about the weather — or even about politics. ("Except," she laughs, "I don't know anything about politics.") She says that she doesn't read books at all. She says that people are more interesting as far as she's concerned. And, she says, she doesn't have to wear her glasses when she's talking to people. I have never seen her wear glasses.

"Now, Bill," she said to me, "there's a couple of things I simply must know. Where are you from?"

"I'm from Indiana," I tell her, although that is a lie. The fact is that I'm from Ohio.

I am most assuredly not named after my father, who had the unique distinction of dying twice. The first time was the year of my birth and was, so I was told, the result of an automobile accident "in the west". That was a lie.

The second story came out in jumps and gasps of self-vindication when I was seven years old. Even then it was difficult for my mother to justify her earlier prevarications, although, to be fair about it, she had not ever told me in so many words that my father had been killed in an automobile accident in the west. She had merely talked *about* the fact to her friends (the Magees, among others), and had allowed me to infer that, on a trip west, my father had run his Graham-Paige off the road (Where? In New Mexico, as I pictured it, or closer home, in Missouri?) and had been crumpled amid the resulting crush of the old car. "Such a *tragedy*," murmured Mrs. Magee, from out of her tough and sinewy face. "Such a tragedy." Then she and my mother looked away from one another as if to agree to understand. It was clearly the result of his *drinking*, because, as I was given to understand from the words of a number of preachers who marched through our lives like issuings from the Book-of-the-Month Club, death was the result of *drinking*.

So be it. Amen.

But when my father was killed a second time, the circumstances made the situation more obscure—at first—and finally somewhat awkward because it became clear that *someone was lying somewhere*.

It happened this way. I had been playing in the back room, in the little shed which led off the back room, and where Mother kept her wash-tubs, etc. I was practising what I took to be the manual of arms because I had just learned that war had broken out somewhere or other (it was vague, but WE HAD BEEN ATTACKED) and I was preparing for war. I vaguely resented the idea of war because I was under the impression that *I would have to do as I was told.* That is, I would have to carry my rifle (I had my toy shotgun) in just this manner, and no other. I was offended by the belief that further etiquette would be demanded of me. I did not like etiquette.

"Will I have to hold my gun just like this?"

"I suppose a soldier must do as he is told," my mother said.

"And will I have to shoot it just like this?" I devised an impossibly awkward position, and made as if to fire my weapon.

"War is a terrible thing," she said.

It is perhaps important that I had no qualms whatever about killing people. *Killing*, death, had not yet permeated my consciousness.

However, at that moment Mrs. Magee came rushing into the house and Mother went rushing out to greet her, and before Mother could shush her, the words were blurted out: "Did you know that Johnny has been killed?" There was a suitable pause, and then Mrs. Magee said what she had wanted to say and what in fact she had come to say. "I suppose it's a blessing to have him really dead at last." Then she went on to talk about how Mother was "free at last", and perhaps "Little Billy can have a real father, one who can stay sober . . . you're still young enough to remarry."

"Yes . . . I guess so," said Mother. And then she saw me, standing at attention as if I were on official sentry duty by the door.

"Oh," said Mrs. Magee, and it seemed to me that she was gone in a wink, because then Mother was kneeling down beside me and speaking to me very carefully (this indicated that the matter was of Supreme Importance), telling me that she was very sorry, and she regretted the necessity, only I wouldn't have understood, but she had not told me the truth — the *real* truth — about my father.

And what was the real truth? Oh, it didn't come out for years, and then only in dribbles and droplets, and generally after a sermon which my mother found particularly touching. But it came out that my father, John Boyd, was a hard-drinking man. (At first I pictured him as a tall, suave character, something like Clark Gable, who drank in his films and whom women seemed to find dangerously alluring. But that was wrong. John Boyd was a short, tough little man who got drunk on pay-day. The veins in his nose "were all broken".)

Well enough. "And?" I asked my mother, in all innocence, not having the slightest idea why she was so upset, but sensing that some sort of advantage was to be gained by pressing onward.

Mother was a fairly large woman. She couldn't stay down on her knees very long; even at church. She rose and shuffled around.

"He was working with some men—tearing down an old shack."

Indeed. John Boyd was a casual labourer who would work at any job long enough to get himself a bottle.

"They were loading some logs on a truck."

"Yes?"

She tried to invoke a few sobs here, from out of the depths of her sadness, but there were no sobs there. "The log spun on top of the load," she said. "It came around on him with great force. He seemed to see it but was not able to duck in time."

Ah. Drunk, no doubt, I concluded. Undoubtedly drunk—too drunk to be able to duck. He stood there on the bed of the truck and watched as the great log—a beam perhaps?—spun around on the top of the load, and paralysed by the sudden advent of his own death, and drunk in the bargain, small, tough John Boyd, who spent money on drink as fast as he earned it, who deserted my mother the year I was born, was felled as surely as if he had been an ox and had been felled by a farmer swinging a log into the dense space between his eyes. Dead.

Mother put on her apron and prepared supper for us. I returned to reading *Life* magazine and looking at pictures of the war. In the evening Mrs. Magee came by to "sit with" Mother, and afterwards we all went to church, where everyone was very considerate of Mother and avoided me—naturally enough. It would have been awkward to talk to me ("How much does the boy know?"), and furthermore, I was the only living result of John Boyd, who was a drunk and a fool.

But the church was a comfort to Mother, and not only in the sense that it put its stamp of righteousness on everything she did. It also gave her a sense of being useful, because Mother was always engaged to be secretary and/or treasurer of this or that committee. She kept the money in a small square box in her drawer in the bureau (right above my socks), and she always wrote the amount which was supposed to be *in* the box on the top of the box and crossed out the last amount. She counted it some evenings. I watched.

But Mother went up in the world. She was a very fine elementary-school teacher; she had a "sweet" disposition, and she was always praised for her hard work, and her ex-pupils always remembered her kindly and sometimes stopped her on the street to say, joyfully, "I'll bet you don't remember me." She would put her finger to her lips, look carefully at the fellow, and then remember his name. He would be pleased and then at a loss for conversation, and would drift off, saying "Well . . . keep up the good work, Mrs. Boyd." But, as she went up in the world, as she got better and better teaching positions and the one-room school disappeared into history to be replaced by proper brick grade-schools, so we went up in our choice of churches.

It is a common enough phenomenon. Perhaps you have noted it. One's God may be the same, but He certainly changes His personality as the congregation achieves financial status.

At first, for example, we went to the Pentecostal Promise Church in Burtonville. Burtonville was not much of a town, and the church was not much of a building. In fact, it was only the basement of a building, and the first floor had been roofed over, an oil space-heater had been installed, the front had been done up with a proper ecclesiastical notice-board and asphalt imitation-brick, and chairs had been acquired from a recently deceased undertaker and still had the words BURTON'S FUNERAL HOME stencilled on them.

There was no regular preacher. There was simply the congregation (which had signed for the mortgage under the leadership of the wealthiest member), and the "services" were generally prayer-meetings and hymn-singings which were punctuated by testimonials. How we loved to wash our dirty linen in public, which we called "cleansing ourselves of sin". It was glorious to hear the pathetic little confessions. "I was mean to my Ma," was a favourite. And this would be repeated and repeated (verbal facility was not noticeably prevalent in the congregation) until weeping took place. Then everyone felt better.

But sometimes there were visiting evangelists who came through. And more often than not, the evangelists specialized in some sort of "faith-healing".

When I asked my mother what faith-healers *did*, she replied, simply enough, that they cured people through faith, and I asked her why they didn't open an office or a clinic like regular doctors. Why don't they stay *here*? Mother replied that they "just didn't". She gave me *that look*, which implied that it was their bounden duty to wander the whole of America, doing small miracles for aches and pains.

And once—we were just about to "move on" and upward to a new church, but I didn't know that, of course—I asked her if she—a *schoolteacher*—actually believed in all that—the faith-healing and the miracles.

Mother, doing something with her hands which meant that she couldn't look directly at me (she was always doing something with her hands which meant that she couldn't look directly at me), said that she believed in the Miracle of Christ.

But no, I insisted. That was not what I meant. *Did she believe in the miracles of Brother Luke and Brother John*—who happened to be the healers who were in town at the time?

She replied that they seemed to do some people some good, and that was good enough for her. They *relieved* suffering, she said.

Yes, I said. But did they *cure* it?

They did God's work, she said.

But were the people actually cured? Was there no more pain?

They did God's will, she insisted. I did not notice the distinction she made.

And that evening we descended into the Pentecostal Promise Church to witness the faith of Brother Luke and Brother John. It was a cool evening, and when the space-heater was turned up there was a sudden heavy aroma of damp, none-too-clean wool. James Magee and his wife drove us to the meeting. We all scrunched up in the front of his Ford pick-up truck.

Brother Luke and Brother John worked as a team and, contrary to all expectation, they were actually brothers. That is, they did not merely call one another "brother" as they called my mother "sister", for example, but were actually blood-brothers, and looked it. They had nearly identical, distinctive straight black hair, for one thing, and piercing black eyes. Perhaps they had Indian — or Oriental — blood in them somewhere. Indeed, perhaps they were twins.

And they both wore black suits, white shirts, and black ties. Their faces were pale, and they did not smile. And it was shortly evident that they shared a technique as well.

It was simplicity itself. They did not move. That was the technique. They stood straight and tall as statues and emitted their utterances, and revealed no expression whatever.

That in itself was unique.

But although they worked as a team, they attacked different manifestations of the devil.

Brother Luke preached first. He spoke against Drink, by which he meant all spiritous liquors down to and including beer and wine. Such beverages, he was to warn us, robbed the nerves, and reduced all men to the attitudes and behaviour of swine. This struck me as reasonable.

But I have rushed ahead. What actually happened was in the mode of a *performance.* The church was dark enough, but it was darkened further by drawing the curtains. Then candles were lit on either side of the plywood pulpit. The deacon hurried through his usual announcements (the church supper, the coming prayer meeting, the study group which was to meet at our house), and announced simply that Brother Luke and Brother John would speak in turn for the Glory of Christ the Son of God.

The deacon disappeared, and Brother Luke stood between the candles.

"Drink," he announced. (You may be sure there were no giggles.)

"Drink," he continued, "is a sin and anyone who denies it is already damned to wrestle forever in Hell. His good soul will wrestle with his evil soul, but the evil soul will have already won here on earth."

"Drink," he made the point, "is hell on earth."

I noticed some nodding in agreement among the congregation, although my mother, evidently by an act of will, kept her head bowed, but unmoving.

Then Brother Luke launched into his speciality – his own unique testimonial to the power of Christ – which was that he *was able to speak without punctuation*. This must be distinguished, of course, from "speaking in tongues", which is quite a different thing altogether and, indeed, is somewhat common. A good evangelist has an individual style.

Brother Luke simply spoke without punctuation, and I sat as enthralled as everyone else, wondering how he could do it without drawing a breath. He said:

"Drink drowns the mind which is the agent of the soul which is the agent of the angels who are the agents of Christ who is the Son of God sent to save us from the sins which crawl up from the earth to infect our bodies like the diseases of the lower animals and the moss which grows over boulders and trees and the rust which infects the crops like beetles and destroys their being and is like drink which infects first the body and then the mind and then the soul and is therefore an affront to the angels who are the agents of Christ who is the Son of God."

Somebody said "Amen", and he caught his breath and went on. However, I thought that he must have developed some sort of trick whereby he could speak with the air coming *in* over his voice box as well as out. It was remarkable.

Had I had any young friends my age I would surely have cornered them after the performance to ask them: "Did *you* see him breathe in? I didn't, but did you?" But I had no friends my age, and when I asked my mother she simply ignored the question — which meant that she disapproved of it, and therefore I was upon forbidden ground. There was only the sidelong glance (while her hands did something important with her apron or a bowl) which meant: *Don't upset Mother.*

When he finished his breathless oratory (where would he have been if we had not said "Amen"?) Brother Luke asked the congregation to stand and vow not to drink, and, in the dark and silence, we did.

When some years later I took my first forbidden drink of beer, I was pleased to discover how *bitter* it was, and loved it the more for that.

But after all, Brother Luke had dealt only in preventative medicine, as it were. He warned us, and predicted dire consequences. He seemed only, *merely*, reasonable. But it was *Brother John* who had the task of repairing obvious calamity and, furthermore, dealing with the clear manifestations of the Devil. It was *Brother John* who was the *Healer*, and thus, the star of the show.

To his credit, Brother John claimed to be able to cure only those illnesses *caused* by the Devil. As someone later remarked, "He wasn't no use at all against a corn-picker," which could slice off your hand.

Brother John's technique, although it was similar to Luke's, was not the same. He was seen to breathe. In fact, he gulped in air like a drowning man. But he served as a complement to his brother, who had already warmed up the audience.

One shadow departed – that was Brother Luke. Another shadow slipped in and became pale flesh: that was Brother John.

A whisper appeared in the air. "Do you believe?"

Almost no one heard him because his voice was so low, so quiet. And we leaned forward to hear. Again he said: "Do you believe?" But this time, I swear, we did *not* hear it, although we felt the impress of his words on the air. We were in agony. He was speaking to us, and we could not hear the Word of God.

"Do you believe?" he said again, and this time we did hear him, and there were little scattered murmurs of assent. But these did not please him. He spoke again. "Do you believe?" And now, knowing what was expected of us, we replied, quite nearly in unison, "Yes." He paused, staring out at us and beyond us, through us, and said again: "Do you believe?" And we said "Yes." Our reply was firm.

"Is Christ the Son of God?" he asked.

"Yes," we answered.

"And the Saviour of the World?"

"Yes," we said.

"And the Power and the Glory?"

"Yes," we said.

And now he was increasing the speed of his delivery and raising the pitch of his voice and, with it, the loudness of his voice, until he was standing there as rigid as a statue and screaming at us: "Do you believe that Christ can heal you?"

And what could one say but "Yes"? And then "Yes" again and "Yes" again. He had us.

But then, Corrie, a terrible thing happened. We were all

in such a pitch of salvation that, had I thought of it, I would have feared that I would wet myself (a constant worry), when Brother John called for those with illnesses of the Devil to come forward to be cured by the words of Christ.

But the first man to step forward was Albert Bruner, and Albert Bruner's affliction was a dead eye. That is, his eye was still in its socket and even moved in union with the good eye, but it saw nothing.

And had the Brothers Luke and John known the nature of Albert Bruner's affliction I am sure that they would have asked him to come for private prayer, as they do in particularly difficult cases, but the fact is that Albert Bruner also *limped*, and they must have thought that he was coming forward to be cured of arthritis, a common enough affliction of the Devil and one with which Brother John had had some success. Indeed, there were a number of brethren present whose gnarled limbs were already loosening into youth in sheer anticipation.

But it was Albert Bruner who stepped up and bowed his head under the uplifted chin of Brother John. Bruner said: "My eye."

"What?" said Brother John, not moving an inch or showing the least emotion or even reaction.

"My eye."

For a moment – yes, for a moment I thought that I saw a tightening of horror in Brother John's jaw, as if he were being insulted by a Disbeliever who had somehow crept in, disguised as a sad, sorry old fellow.

But Albert Bruner muttered. "My eye. I'm blind in my eye."

There was nothing to do but pray for a Miracle.

And therefore Brother John prayed. He called upon the angels in their multitudes and Christ in particular to take time from their many duties to look after this one sparrow, and he pleaded – indeed, he *did* plead – with Christ.

But Bruner was stubbornly honest. Brother John spoke

very slowly, giving Albert Bruner the chance to consider every word. "Brother, do you *feel* even a glimmer of light?"

Bruner shook his head in the negative.

"Please," said Brother John. "Do you *feel* a *presence* of light?"

But Albert Bruner, who had heard clearly the first time, said: "I can't see nothing out of my blind eye."

Brother John, we saw, was in tears. Tears were running down the lean, hard lines of his face which was still directed at the beyond, and when they dripped off his jaw and disappeared into the shadows at his feet, I thought I could hear them fall.

But still Albert Bruner was blind.

Then Brother John lost control of himself. Because he felt that either God or Albert Bruner—or both—was mocking him, he turned savage. He said that Albert Bruner was a sinner, an unrepentant sinner, and was therefore beyond the call of Christ. It was the only thing he *could* do.

Brother John shouted at him: "Are you a sinner?"

We knew our cue. We shouted: "Yes!"

Poor old Bruner, who clerked up at Burton's Hardware, began to weep and denied that he was a sinner. "I ain't no sinner," he wept. Indeed, he had had no more chance to become a sinner in his life than has a child of five.

But then Brother John was gone. Perhaps I blinked my eyes for a moment, but when I looked again, there was no sign, or shadow, of the fierce, dark-haired figure between the tall candles. There was only Albert Bruner on his knees before the congregation.

And then—worst of all—Bruner turned to look at his brothers and sisters in Christ. But so great was his faith, so great I tell you, Corrie, that he turned to look *with his blind eye*! It was large, terrible, and blank.

The meeting ended, you understand, in shuffles and uncertainty. Someone turned on the electric lights and everyone was suddenly very busy looking at coats and purses, and someone must have blown out the candles, and somehow or other (none of us looked) Bruner must have gotten up from his ridiculous position in front of the plywood pulpit and left. No one looked around for Brother Luke and Brother John to talk to them, privately-like, or to invite them home for a bit of late supper, something they "just happened to have in the stove and needed eating up".

Nor do I know if Albert Bruner ever went back to the Pentecostal Promise Church, although I certainly hope that he did not. We moved the next week, in fact, to Clifton, where my mother had "some people" (who were soon to become "relatives", if you catch the distinction), and where Mother had been hired to teach the second grade because the previous teacher had passed away unexpectedly from terminal cancer.

We had not been in Clifton more than a week before Mother said to me one day while she was washing some dishes we never used (to be put away never to be used) that she thought, in Clifton, we might "try the Baptist Church".

Indeed, I was very shortly made aware of how we had moved up in the world. Suddenly my mother was no longer doing her laundry over a scrub-board in the back room; we lived in an apartment now, over the *Clifton 5¢ to $1*, and there was a used Maytag washing machine on the back porch over the loading platform which gave onto the alley. Mother was able to buy herself some decent clothes, and now she wore proper nylon stockings even on Saturday when she stayed home to luxuriate among our laundry. When I asked her why she did not wear the low white socks she used to, her glance was quick and to the point: I was not to ask that.

And now that she had some decent clothes, it became somehow natural that she wanted to keep some secrets for herself. She liked the old Pentecostal people. They were good people. I was to understand that. But look—didn't I like the Baptist Church? (It was an ordinary, standard wooden church building, but you knew that it was a Church. Didn't it have a steeple?)

Yes, and Mother now had no urge whatever to confess her desire for some of the world's goods. Why should she? She had them.

And here beginneth the reign of the Reverend E.B. Dobbs, who exercised over my mother (and me) a most awe-full hold, because he was *successful*. We did not know it when we shuffled into the little church and found it crammed with worshippers, but that was to be the last service held in the little white church on the corner. Within a month it had been razed, and it was erased without a trace. In its place there appeared a flat field of asphalt, marked with yellow lines – the parking lot for Colglazier's IGA Supermarket. Yet this was only half the measure of the Reverend E.B. Dobbs' success.

Because, on the other side of town (and we were soon there, huddled in the vestibule with the rest of the congregation, who already knew my mother as the kindly widow with the gangly son), there rose the real achievement of the Reverend E.B. Dobbs. It was a large church, made of vari-coloured sandstone, with abstract-design stained glass windows. Connected to the church building itself was a wing which contained the Sunday School classrooms, and they were as well-equipped (even better, actually) as the classrooms of the Clifton School System. There was a refrigerated water-fountain in the hallway.

The Reverend E.B. Dobbs was a squat man. He wore a blue suit on all occasions. As he became accustomed to the marks of his own success, the suits became a darker shade of blue. He wore rimless glasses. He was bald. He looked at you with the efficiency of a modern accountant, and he knew your soul as a good psychologist might.

Because I might as well tell the truth: he was a popular clergyman. His sermons were full of common sense. When he criticized his congregation for their wrong-doings (drink, lust, sloth) he did so with a sure hand: he made sure that we were going to agree with him. He disarmed us with jokes and anecdotes — and sometimes his face would break into a genial smile beneath the large, rimless glasses. He rarely talked about Sin except in terms of the Old Testament. To us he talked about our Mistakes.

He admitted his own readily enough. He had worked his way through Divinity School as a telephone repairman, and he often mentioned the difficulty of getting a "direct line", or the frequency and inexplicability of "crossed lines". You never felt *guilty* with the Reverend E.B. Dobbs, although you often felt that you had made a number of mistakes you ought not to have made.

When he said: "Consider the consequences," he was not speaking of the eternal damnation of your soul. He was talking about the disgrace of having made a fool of yourself and finding it necessary to marry somebody you did not even like. "Think," he said. And we all remembered the little motto on his desk in his office. It said THIMK. Of course.

When he played the occasional game with the church softball team he showed himself to be surprisingly adept. There was a rumour that he had once been considered a professional prospect by the Cincinnati Redlegs. He did not disabuse anyone of this rumour, although he did not assist in its propagation either.

It was in the Reverend E.B. Dobbs' Church that I first saw a choir wearing choir robes. They were white, with gold facing.

When I heard the congregation rise and sing with the choir — HOLY, HOLY, HOLY — I found myself looking upward at the varnished beams above the choir-loft, and felt my heart yearning toward glory, and as I joined in with my crude alto, I felt warm all over. I admired Reverend Dobbs nearly to distraction and would have followed him anywhere (so I thought), and indeed, it was the constant fear of the congregation that he would be called elsewhere. Hadn't he accomplished his duty here? Had not he built his church? Had not the congregation increased threefold?

I wanted to sing in the choir, but my mother dissuaded me, saying my voice was not yet ready. "Wait until it finishes changing," she said. It never seemed to, somehow. And Mother gave me one of her few sly and knowing smiles. "I'll bet you just want to sing in the choir so you can sit next to Katherine Dobbs," she said. She was referring to Reverend Dobbs' daughter. She was quite right – and at that time, Katherine Dobbs (blonde, slender, poised) seemed quite out of reach.

If I went to see the Reverend E.B. Dobbs in his office, he always leaned back in his soft swivel chair and asked me how I was, and told me jokes. And when he asked me if he could help me in any way – was anything wrong – I said, "No," and he continued to tell me jokes. "Doing well in school?" I was doing very well indeed, thank you. "So Katherine tells me." The interview invariably ended with his phrase, "Well, I'd better get back to work," and, "Give your mother my regards – and my thanks." He didn't know what he would do with such a large congregation if it were not for the help of my mother and women like her, who "took the meetings" and taught Sunday School.

But what I wanted, you see, was to be of some service to Christianity. I had not told him of my decision because I was afraid he would have *smiled* at me and said, "Wait." But I could not wait. I wanted to be of service.

Very well, then, I decided. I would have to make my own way. If I was not to be taken seriously by the preacher, then I would have to devise a more individualistic method.

The method came to me when I looked upon one of the pamphlets my mother was using to instruct her Sunday School class of nine-to-eleven-year-olds. It was called *The Light of the World*, and it featured a colour reproduction of a print of Christ at the Door to Your Heart. He was in some sort of a garden; there were orange blossoms around the doorway, but there was no door-knob on the door because (as the caption explained) this was the door to your heart, and could only be opened from Within. It was a very warm and cozy picture; it seemed to hint that the acceptance of Christ offered one a whitewashed cottage on the Mediterranean.

And then, on the next page (I had just come home from school and was eating a peanut-butter and jelly sandwich and drinking a glass of milk), there was a short article in simple language which ended with the words in boldface capital letters: LOVE SPREADS LIKE SMILES. Had we not observed that in a room where one person is laughing, others begin to laugh as well? It cannot be helped. It was human nature. Human nature was to be used to spread the word of Christ.

This struck me as perfectly reasonable.

And yet I might have escaped, had I not been (through ill luck—or the power of the Devil) reading Lloyd C. Douglas's books at the time. You will recall, surely, the famous author of *The Magnificent Obsession*? His books were incredibly (if understandably) successful. At this time I had worked back through some of the lesser-known volumes to one called *The Green Light.*

Now, the gist of Lloyd C. Douglas's Christian philosophy was this: you made a deal with God. Of course, it had to be a humble deal—or at least a *secret* one—and if you kept your part of the bargain, God kept His. But you had to do something *selfless*. If you did something *selfless*, then God would *reward* you. The *rewards* were not spelled out explicitly, but they seemed to make you *happy* and *successful*, and they smelled of *money*.

This struck me as a very good deal indeed.

And so the idea struck my puerile consciousness. I would print up (on Mother's spirit-duplicator at the school) a number of SHARES OF LOVE. The *cost* of the Shares would be NOTHING. Yet they would *Pay* the *Bearer Threefold*. I liked phrases like that.

But I wasn't done yet. Each piece of paper would be *One Share of Love,* and on it I would indicate that the Share would INCREASE IN VALUE AS IT WAS PASSED FROM HAND TO HAND.

I actually did it. And I told no one.

I chose a Saturday night for my Revelation. I took the wad of shares in my pocket and told my mother I was going down to the corner for an ice-cream cone. I walked out into a warm summer night. There were visions in my stupid little head. I could see headlines:

W. BOYD CONVERTS
THOUSANDS TO CHRIST

There would be a photograph of me of course, with my mother and the Reverend E.B. Dobbs in the background.

Or: **Boy Evangelist**
Begins Religious
Fervor in Ohio

William A. Boyd, the son of Mrs. John Boyd, Clifton, is attracting wide notice with his inspired ideas and preaching in this small rural community. Local clerics have cautiously compared him to the Child Christ astounding the Elders.

Rev. E.B. Dobbs, pastor of the First Baptist Church, said that the boy is remarkably promising.

Everybody in the surrounding area came in to Clifton on a Saturday night. The cars and pick-up trucks were nosed in along the curb, and while the young people walked up one side of Main Street and down the other, the parents sat in their cars and watched until, at about 9 o'clock, they took their turn. It was almost as if there were an agreement. First the people in the cars on the south side of the street got out, and walked along, crossed the street, and down the north side, stopping from time to time to chat with their friends. "How's the hogs?" or "How's the chickens?" And inquiries were made about the uncertain health of certain friends and relatives. Then, when they had all settled back into their cars, the other group, on the north side, would get out and walk around. The teen-agers hung around in front of the Soda Shop, drinking cokes out of paper cups and eating ice-cream, teasing one another. A boy would run out of the group, a girl would squeal, and the group would break up, only to re-group a few seconds later.

Of course I did not have the courage (or the foolhardiness) to start my revival in front of the Soda Shop. Instead, I went down the street to the unfashionable corner, in front of the Bargain Shoe Store. Nobody but the poor country people ever bought their shoes there. We bought ours from Evans' Shoe Store, which was next to the Morris Furniture Store. There was no street-light in front of the Bargain Shoe Store. There was a driveway which ran behind the shoe store.

I planted myself in the middle of the sidewalk and prepared to become famous.

When the first couple came toward me—a young farmer and his wife—I held out my SHARES OF LOVE toward them. He was a tall man, and the top of his head was a deathly white from having been protected all day from the sun by a hat. When his wife perceived me gesturing toward them, she crumpled into his side, and suddenly the both of them seemed to find great interest in the offerings of the Bargain Shoe Store. I said: "I offer you the Love of Christ—Free," but they turned and crossed the street without waiting until they came to the corner—and me.

And indeed, as long as I stood my ground in the middle of the sidewalk, the walking people avoided me. All by myself I had curtailed the evening strolling circle of Clifton. I stepped back into the shadows, and darted out to thrust my deal with Christ on the passers-by. Most of them simply looked the other way. When I caught some older man — usually a farmer who was thinking about something else — he simply took the SHARE OF LOVE, glanced at it, and shoved it in his pocket.

And I should have seen what was coming because, after all, I was thirteen years old by this time, and if I was something of a solitary boy, nobody had ever accused me of being ignorant. But when I saw this fellow ambling down the street — somewhat more slowly than usual — I thought that I had my first genuine investor in Love. He was about sixteen years old, I should guess, and very well muscled from his work in the fields. He was tanned; he obviously did not wear a hat in the fields. He was wearing blue jeans and a white T-shirt. One arm of the T-shirt was rolled back to hold a pack of cigarettes.

"I'll have one of them," he said.

I was pleased to tender him one of my lovingly made investment slips. He read it carefully and looked at me. I must have been a sorry sight in those days: too large for my clothes; too small for my eyes and my haircut.

Then he ambled back to the gang in front of the Soda Shop. I looked up the street to see the reaction, and saw that the slip was being passed around. The three girls who were with the group were somehow manoeuvred into the background. I began to see myself as the Saviour of Modern Youth.

And as bad luck would have it, there was suddenly a large group of people approaching me: the stores had closed and these were the Morris Furniture Store employees who were just leaving together, and they had parked their cars around the corner by the little One-Stop Grocery. They hadn't been warned about me, and consequently they were not avoiding me, and I hurtled into their midst with my little epistles of love; and because I was occupied with them, I did not notice the tall boy and his buddies come around the back of the Bargain Shoe Store. I was safe with the employees of the Morris Furniture Store, but when they had gone (I was looking after them), I felt myself grabbed by rough hands, and hands were put over my eyes and . . .

And the usual indignity. "De-pants him!" one called. "De-pants him!" I was. I was de-pantsed.

They must have borrowed one of their girl-friends' lipsticks, because, when they had dragged me sobbing into the alley by the Bargain Shoe Store and pulled my pants and shorts down to my ankles, they took the lipstick and made designs all over my belly and private parts.

"Whee-o!" one chortled while I wept.

"Well, I can't hardly *see* the damn thing," said another.

Then, while one kept his huge hand over my eyes, another spread the lipstick on my lips.

And then they were gone.

My Shares of Love were scattered all over the sidewalk in front of the Bargain Shoe Store.

I ran home weeping, and my mother said, "Billy, Billy, what have you *done*?"

I screamed at her. "I haven't done *any*thing. *They* did it to *me*."

She filled the tub for me and I stripped off my clothes and threw my underwear in the trash. I got into the tub, still weeping.

Mother called from outside. "They're bullies, Billy. That's all. They're just bullies."

I wept.

"Most people are bullies," she said.

And it was true. When I went to see the Reverend E.B. Dobbs in his fine, fancy office the next day he tried to be sympathetic — and he actually had one of my Shares of Love in his hands — but he said: "Look here, Bill, Christianity is not some kind of Captain Midnight game."

"You haven't got any faith!" I shouted at him, but he just smiled, pleased with himself, and repeated (and repeated again at a sermon later, only thankfully, not the next

Sunday) that "Christianity isn't a Captain Midnight game."

"You haven't a bit of faith in Christ!" I yelled at him, but he simply ignored me and said, "And now I guess you'll just have to endure it," and I did. I endured it, but I learned to hate that sleazy hypocrite, the Reverend E.B. Dobbs, although I concealed it well enough to marry his daughter.

Because, having slipped scornfully through Indiana Teachers College as quietly as possible, I came back to Clifton to pay court to Katherine Dobbs. Why not? She offered me what I thought was satisfaction.

First of all, she was a promising beauty; which is to say that she had all the offerings of an excellent and firm bosom, an upright carriage, and a certain shyness which is easily mistaken for flirtation. Yet she was not so beautiful that she had a large number of followers. Consequently, she was not so beautiful that she could laugh at me. My vivid imagination did the rest.

I imagined what she would be like under the pale pink dress she wore that summer.

We "courted" at "church socials". Such quaint terms for the ritual circling of lust.

She seemed to find my earnestness a promising sign. I believe she saw herself (in me) as the Wife of the Superintendent of Schools.

But when she turned her head away at some comment of mine which she thought not quite proper, my eyes devoured her bosom with a frankness which would have brought a gleam to the eye of Saint Paul. Oh, I burned, I tell you, I burned.

Mother, too, was quite pleased with the prospects of the union. She said that Katherine and I looked "quite nice together". That was sufficient for Mother, who judged people always on their Sunday behaviour. "Katherine dresses so cleverly—so well." Yes, that was true, and since Mother's liberation from the Pentecostals, she thought quite highly of what she thought was "good taste", which, in fact, she gleaned by looking through and through the Sears-Roebuck catalogue.

When I looked at Katherine — or even thought about her — my mind was blinded black by the thought of how I would liberate that body from those clothes, and how I would explore, possess, and play with that body. I had a young man's joy at the thought of fondling the delicious goods.

However, one believed in morality in those days. One wanted to be "good". Being good, we thought, was even better than being ecstatic. We had long earnest talks on the porch, lumped against the wall in the shadow of the lilac bush, and decided to go to our marriage bed as virgins. I think we rather enjoyed fondling one another's pitiful little guilts.

I thought of Katherine as Nude (ah! pink and downy and . . .) and concluded that this must be Love.

Katherine thought of how we looked walking down the street and my good reputation for earnestness, looked into the future which was crowded with the very friends she had then, and thought that this was Love.

The Reverend E.B. Dobbs performed the ceremony. There was a goodly-sized crowd at the church because, although neither of us had many relatives to call upon, the entire congregation was invited by her bountiful father, and the members were pleased to turn out for such a significant occasion. Everyone felt warm and happy — I believe the term is "smug and self-righteous" — without so much as a twinge of guilt. Even I did not have a twinge of guilt. I had just been given licence to handle the yum-yums. I cannot even remember her face.

Following the ceremony we left Clifton for what purported to be the joys of the honeymoon. We were going directly from the honeymoon trip to my first teaching post, and therefore would not be back in Clifton until the Christmas holidays. We went in the second-hand 1948 Ford

Coupe I had purchased with great care.

It did not work very well either.

Katherine, it turned out, was given to deeper weepings than I had imagined. I suspected that she might be a little "virginal", but I did not imagine that she would be so determined about it. She cried the first night and I soothed her; she cried the second night and I sympathized with her. She cried the next afternoon just thinking about the coming night and I told her to go to hell.

By the time we reached the end of our honeymoon the marriage was over. I snarled at her, and she wept. It was the end, we agreed. And then we made the mistake of agreeing that we really ought to try to "work things out together".

By this Katherine meant that she would try to capture as nearly as possible her previous virginity, which seemed to entail the purchase of a large amount of clothes which we could ill afford. I remonstrated. She than returned from her next shopping expedition with clothes for me as well as clothes for herself. She held up the gorgeous sweater she had bought as if it were a true gift. "Isn't it beautiful?" She would make me a virgin, too.

"It is beautiful but we cannot afford it."

"But I bought it for you."

"Thank you, but I neither want it nor need it."

She hadn't the faintest idea of the value of a dollar. She bought clothes as naturally as she purchased food, and with equally little thought as to value received for money given.

And the thought of sex made her faint. "Look here," I said to her, "do you think that marriage is some kind of eternal card-party, where we sit around and *look* at one another and simper from time to time?"

She began to sniffle.

"Marriage is the union of Meat!" I shouted at her, and she howled.

Until the marriage ended I never did see her in less than

a slip and a bra. She locked the door when she was bathing. She moved from street-clothes to night-gown (opaque, of course) like some kind of magic butterfly, and I never saw the stages of development.

I did not swear at her the day I left her. It was dawn, I'd had a sleepless night, and I was tired. I simply rose from our bed (she had wept herself to sleep again), and I said: "You are a moth," and I left. I do not believe she awoke.

But I was right. She was a moth. Nothing more if nothing less.

When she filed suit (tearfully, I should imagine) for divorce, she testified that I made fun of her friends to their faces. Well, I would not have chosen those grounds, but for what it was worth—she was quite right. I did take a certain pleasure in telling her idiot friends that there were three kinds of people in this world: fools, absolute fools, and total dolts, and that they were bucking for admission to the final category. It made for quiet bridge games. Their faces fell. I did not contest the divorce. I simply moved on.

Now Corrie is coming closer. The washing machine has ceased its trembling hum and is shuddering to a halt. There is a heavy silence as she approaches, walking gracefully in a tease to repeat her question.

"What did you say? I didn't hear you. Where are you from?"

"I'm from Indiana," I lie.

She is now right before me on the other side of the grill, and I feel, rather, that she is pushing me and challenging me to stand up very straight and be rough. But she is laughing.

"And now,"—she interrupts herself to laugh with feigned embarrassment—"I *have* to ask, Bill—were you ever married?"

Just like Dorah Garrett in this one single respect.

"No," I say, "I have never married."

Then I hear Tennie bellow from above, roaring thinly like a man who wishes to be King: "Hey, Corrie, goddammit, what are you *do*ing down there? Come *on*."

Without so much as a further word, she goes to him.

When she was gone I found myself staring at the squat, ungainly white washing machine, over against the far wall. And then I looked more closely, concentrated my attention, in fact, on the grill in front of me. I could easily cut a door through the rough lattice-work. If I used a small saw-blade, I could do it so neatly that it would never be noticed, and then I would be able to slip over there in the dark of night.

It is the season's first snowfall. It is a heavy, thick snow, and it covers everything with a thick blanket. When I look out my window at Howard Street I notice only the two parallel tracks where a single car has made its way out. Somebody has had to go to work.

Fredericton is snuggled under the snow. Then the sun comes out and illuminates the town. The light seems to get *inside* the town and brightens it up, like *crystal*, or, quaintly, like a Christmas card.

It is perhaps rather tawdry.

I met Corrie when I was trudging back from town that morning. She was pulling Robert in the little sled I had given him. I bought a cheap sled on sale at Canadian Tire, and bolted on a wooden box (I found it abandoned in the basement), and painted the entire contraption blue. "Look how beautifully it works," Corrie called out to me. We walked back together. After a while I offered to pull Robert, but Corrie insisted that she could do it quite well.

"Would you like to come for a cup of coffee?" she said, when we were home.

"Do you really mean it?" I asked.

"Of *course* I mean it," she said.

She put Robert down for a little nap, but he didn't want to go to sleep. She insisted, he protested, and it was necessary for her to spank him before she could have her way. I waited quietly in the living-room.

Then she was back and in the kitchen making the coffee. She was singing. A Beatles song, I believe: "Hey Jude". She has a true voice, but it lacks power and conviction.

She put the coffee in front of me and sat in the chair opposite me. We did not speak for several moments.

"It's very quiet, isn't it?" she said suddenly.

"Yes it is," I agreed.

"I like it. America was very noisy, wasn't it?"

"Yes." Then I added: "The only difficulty is deciding what to do with the silence."

"What to do with it?"

"Nature abhors a silence as it abhors a vacuum."

"Oh," she said, perplexed. But she brightened. "I like it, though," she said. "I come from a large family—there were ten of us—and there was never much silence, so . . . "

"How did you meet Tennie?" I interrupted.

"Meet Tennie?"

"Yes."

"Oh. Well," she began, sipping at her coffee (quickly and delicately, like a cat), "we met at a summer camp."

"Yes?"

"Yes," she continued. "I was waiting tables at this summer camp to earn some money to go to college, and Tennie—well, Tennie had already graduated—had his B.A., you know—and was working for the summer to get some money for graduate school in the fall. He had a fellowship, of course, but he wanted to earn a bit of spending money. We got married at the end of summer. That's why I never went to college. It was at Camp Watahatchee, in Michigan. A private camp."

She waited for me to say something, but I did not, so she

told me that she had planned to go to college eventually, after they "got settled", but now she didn't feel much like it.

She was a bit of a tomboy, she said. Did I know that?

I told her that I had suspected it. "How?" she asked. I replied that I reached my conclusion from her habitual apparel of blue jeans and sweatshirt, and she laughed.

"Yes," she said. She pulled her long hair into make-believe pigtails and gave me a toothy, idiotic grin.

Did I know, she wondered, that in her day she was the best centre-fielder in her neighbourhood. Boy *or* girl?

No, I had not known that.

Well she was, she said. At age twelve.

"Do you think that we ought to have a fence put up?" I said.

"A fence?"

"Yes."

"You mean—like the Garretts suggested—to keep my children off your half of the lawn?"

No, no, I hastened to reassure her. I meant something quite different. I thought that perhaps I ought to have a fence constructed around the entire property.

"It would keep people from throwing their trash in the yard," I said. "Out there right now, under that snow, there are probably ten empty pop bottles."

"You don't like those non-returnable bottles, do you?" she said.

"They ought to be banned," I said.

"Yes," she agreed. Still, they *were* convenient.

"The aesthetic cost of convenience is too high," I said.

"Yes," she said. "Well, if you put a fence up then I could put Robert out to play and not worry about him."

"Yes," I said. "It would give us more privacy."

She agreed.

I told her that I was thinking of a chain-link fence, with some kind of plant growing on it.

"Uh-uh," she said. "That's no good. We had one like that once when we were living in Illinois. And the plant pulled it down."

Yes, I could see how that might happen.

"And the snow pushes against it as well," she said.

Yes, I could see that.

"Not for this climate," she laughed. Why didn't I consider one of those woven-wooden things. It would mean more privacy, she said.

It wouldn't last as long as a chain-link fence, I suggested.

"Well," she said, "nothing lasts, but wood is better." She grinned at me. "Remember?"

Then she looked out the window and spied Jack and Alisha coming home from school. "Oh, damn," she said. "It's lunch-time already. Want to stay for lunch?"

"No thank you."

"All right. Just *look* at them."

Alisha was already in tears of exasperation because Jack was chasing her and throwing snowballs at her. She was covered with snow, as if in fact he had already knocked her down. We stood at the window, shading our eyes from the sun, and watched the battle as it progressed toward the door. As Alisha rattled in the front door, a snowball hit just beside her, and some of the snow actually spattered inside. Jack was laughing.

Alisha was howling. "Jack is a *bastard*, a *bastard* — look at me!" Her face was red, and she had snow sliding down her neck. She shuddered.

Corrie was shocked, then angry, at her language.

Today Corrie telephoned me. Our phones are back to back because, simply enough, they are installed on opposite sides of our mutual wall, and therefore when I heard her dialling and heard the resulting ring, I knew it was she.

She said she had suddenly had a thought. She had a

perfectly good washing machine down there in the basement, and she could easily do my laundry as well as Tennie's.

I refused, of course. It was a shocking suggestion. It would be the next thing to sharing a toothbrush.

I went downtown.

This is the letter I wrote:

Dear Sir:

Please grant me a small space in your estimable paper to assert an unpopular position "for the time of year". There is no doubt whatever by this time, that "godless materialism" (to use a favourite Sunday phrase) has taken over Western Culture. Nor is it surprising that Christmas should now be a time of blatantly commercial activity. One does not expect the commercial souls of merchants suddenly to remember not only the Gift of Christ to Man, but also his Crucifixion and Resurrection. One expects the merchants to use the occasion to sell their goods; Christianity has become an adjunct to the Winter Sale Catalogue.

But it seems to me that the Clergy, if they had any faith at all in their Calling (or simply a pride in their job), would be out in the streets in protest at this mockery, carrying placards (at the very least) or, remembering the activities of Christ (Matthew 21:12), taking axes to the *tawdry* displays of junk which are being foisted on the unsuspecting public by men who know no motive but profit.

The Clergy have failed in the duty they vowed to do, and deserve, I think, a special Eucharist for this Christmas-time. I would suggest the assembled local Clergy be served a banquet of tiny chicken-hearts skewered on little sticks, served on paper plates with a poinsettia design. They do not deserve our prayers.

Sincerely yours,

William A. Boyd
696 Rodman Street
Fredericton, N.B.

AN ALIEN'S GUIDE TO SURVIVAL (Continued)

It ought to be granted, then, that within limits (his individual inheritance, his bodily limitations, his place of birth, and the fact of death), man has the inalienable right to choose his life. And as it is with an individual man, so is it with mankind. Mankind *chooses* what *a man* is. And, if we take a certain number of men to represent what we call a "culture", then the collective choice results in the personality of the civilization.

However, mankind is now faced with problems of greater magnitude (and consequences) than ever before. Where in earlier, happier times a cultural mistake might result in the deaths of several thousand people, the possibility is now before us that any one of a number of *mistakes* will result in the extinction of Man. I am here referring to the atomic bomb and the problem of ecological suicide, sometimes called pollution. In other words, the results of man's decisions are no longer such minor matters as comfort or discomfort (or that adjunct to idealism — a "better" or "worse" life which results from that which we "ought" or "ought not" to do), but *ultimate death.*

Consequently, we are now faced with the necessity of making a choice of ultimate consequences. Such a choice requires more courage than ever before (more courage than that which is possessed by any popularity-seeking politician, for example), and furthermore requires a *new kind* of decision. We must choose — not to *act* — but to *refuse to act.* In short, we must choose to *reject.*

It is upon this principle of *rejection* that civilization will either *survive* or *destroy itself.*

For example, we must now reject what are referred to by politicians (of both "left" and "right") as "economic realities". These "economic realities" are in fact nothing more than the extensive myths of *industrialization.* (You will notice that not even the most rabid left-winger ever suggests that *all* factories ought to be *destroyed.*) The "economic realist" is concerned only with *jobs,* not with *life.* But it is clear that to choose industrialism is to choose to commit suicide.

Consequently it is clearly evident that we must reject the automobile and all the industry that goes with it. And what if millions of people *are* thrown out of work? It is *their discomfort* versus the *survival of mankind.* Furthermore, we must learn to reject the lust which makes mankind populate itself like rats at the local dump.

And furthermore — and this is more *intrinsic* to my philosophy than you might suppose — we must reject that which is *ugly.* And by *ugly* I mean that which is *offensively temporary.* It is perfectly illustrated by the K-Mart Shopping Plaza (at the top of Smythe Street Hill in Fredericton, New Brunswick). It is self-evident that ugliness debases men. Unless he is made of *very stern stuff* indeed, a man will act under the influence of his surroundings. Put a man in prison — and he will act like a prisoner. Surround a man with the shoddy goods of contemporaneity, and he will act in *proportion to their measure.*

Or perhaps I might make this point more clearly by simply referring to the prevalence of disposable items in our day-to-day lives. We are surrounded by empty tin-cans, plastic milk-bags, cardboard cartons, paper bags, and that most heinous item of all, the non-returnable (disposable) soft-drink bottle. These are items which are manufactured to be of *no value whatever.* But, if we surround man with items of *no value whatever,* it is only a short step to the belief that *man* — or *human life* — is of *no value* whatever. Now we are to have "abortions on demand". Indeed. And shortly we shall have suicides on demand. (It has already been suggested by some Scandinavian social "thinker".) And clearly we now kill people at long range — kill them as abstractly as we turn over the page of their statistics. Nothing has any value anymore. The only value is cash-profit, and this, ironically, is all nothing more than an economic myth to which we have ridiculously agreed to adhere.

You ask me: what is the solution? The solution is courage, of course, and the adoption of the *Principle of Rejection.* But there is also the possibility that a number of men, or even a single man — one of those men of "sterner stuff" whom I mentioned above — will arise to deal with the problem of mankind. They will be "heroes". That is to say, they will act in the *best interests* of *mankind* rather than in their *own narrow ones.* As the ancient medieval knights fared forth to emulate the principles of Christ, so will the Modern Hero go forth to enact the *Principle of Rejection.*

I foresee the rise, in fact, of *Conservation Commandoes,* who will be men dedicated to the destruction of factories, automobiles, and snowmobiles.

Therefore one comes to certain harsh decisions for oneself. Decisions which cannot be escaped because they weigh on the mind like an unpaid debt, like an obligation of honour.

When spring comes I shall gather the bottles which have been thrown on my lawn. I shall even collect the shards of glass of those which have been smashed. Those which are as yet whole I shall smash into a barrel. Then I shall fill a sack with the exploded pieces of glass.

I shall look up the home address of the local soft-drink distributor. If necessary, I shall follow him home from work, stealthily as a footpad.

Then, in the dark of the night I shall go (dressed in dark clothes, with a dark woollen cap over my head, my face blackened with cork) to his home with my load of disposable bottles. Like a thief in the night I shall approach his door, slipping through the shadows from the street-light. Then, with a sudden leap—a twist in the air like a cat leaping after a string—I shall disgorge my sack of broken glass with a resounding tinkle, and leap away into the shadows again. I shall be gone before the evil-doer opens his door to look with astonishment upon the harvest which he has sown.

But he, of course, will call the police. How shall I escape? This is how I shall escape. On my way, I shall go to the nearest service station. It will not be busy—there are too many service stations in the Fredericton area. I shall ask for the key to the men's washroom. In the washroom I shall change into my battle costume and apply the burnt cork to my face. I shall put on a cold-cream base so that it will come off easily. Then I shall go off to commit my gesture, but I shall *keep the key to the washroom* and leave my civilian clothes there.

Therefore, when I come running back (*behind* the filling station) with the howls of the police sirens in the summer's night air, I shall need only to slip into the washroom, remove the burnt cork from my face, change back into my civilian clothes, and saunter forth into the nearest little restaurant or fish'n'chip shop and there mingle with the populace. I shall leave the washroom key in the door.

When I know that Corrie is home alone (with only Robert for small company, or when he is silent in sleep), and I hear the water humming through the pipes, I run upstairs. Usually I am in luck. Corrie is taking a shower.

I put down the lid of my toilet and sit on it, and listen to Corrie sing. Sometimes she sings the terrible old songs of Rodgers and Hammerstein (disgusting slop!) like "I'm Gonna Wash That Man Right Out of My Hair", but on other occasions her taste is better. I am happier when I hear her sweet small voice flowering o'er "Hey Jude".

It has become my habit to accompany Corrie to the York County Market (on George Street) on Saturday morning.

I wait by my window until I see her come out of her door with her shopping basket. Then I take mine and go out my door to join her.

I think that it is fair to say that we have an enjoyable time of it at the market. There is a certain delight in being surrounded by so much rough food. For example, there are heaps of vegetables piled up on the display tables (which the purveyors rent from the market corporation for a nominal fee), and there are sacks of vegetables leaning in lumps against the legs of the display tables. There are sacks of potatoes, and bushel-baskets full of carrots. There are heaps of turnips, parsnips, and stolid displays of that unique gourd-squash: the Turk's Head. And there are apples: McIntosh, Cortland, and Hume (delicious!) from Keswick Ridge. Baskets and boxes of neatly packed eggs. Has God ever designed anything more *perfect* than an egg?

And the meat is piled high and bountiful. There are stacks of red steaks, piles of roasts, gatherings of chops. There are heaps of chickens, packaged for home, ready for the frying-pan or broiler-tray. Occasionally one sees even a whole half of a lamb, for example, and once I saw an entire hog stretched out on a table: it was as pink and innocent as a child—even though it was split up the middle.

And of course the market is the place where country meets town. Here the short, tough old farmers, gnarled as country bushes, with their hats or caps pulled low over their eyes, meet the determinedly elementary custom of the members of the University of New Brunswick faculty. The faculty members are easily identifiable. They dress like country people, although it is clear that these casual clothes are worn only once a week. And they have beards. They endeavour to look like farmers of seventy years ago. But the farmers themselves do not wear beards. (Indeed, I find a beard to be an affectation, a *costume* of independence.) The faculty members are invariably taller than the farmers.

The professors talk to one another and buy from the farmers. The farmers stamp their green mud-boots from habit and grunt at one another in barnyard good humour.

The farm wives are large and shapeless as puddings — as a farm wife ought to be — although the occasional daughter has a remarkable beauty. The country girl has strong thighs and calves, and stands muscularly erect with a stance which indicates that she can laugh at hard work.

It is the men who are broken. The broken old men sit on a green bench between the front door of the market and the canteen. One of them is offensively old, has a bad purple/grey colour, and is so bent that his head is barely above his waist. He rarely hobbles far from the bench. The work and the land have broken him, and if a man must be broken, then this is as it should be.

At the front entrance they are allowed to sell puppies, and Corrie always looks when we come in to see if there are any this particular week. She is always pleased when there are some, and she always asks about them.

"What kind are they?" she says, even as she picks up one bundle of fur and cuddles it.

"They're Labrador and collie."

I doubt she has any idea of how they will turn out. Indeed, it is difficult to imagine the consequences of such chance matings, wild as the weather.

"Aren't you *sweet*!" she says, holding the puppy up at arm's length and smiling at it as if it were a baby (and incidentally, ascertaining its sex). "Yes you *are*," she coos, answering her own question. "You're *sweet*."

When she puts the puppy down and it is returned by its owner to the cardboard box, she invariably remarks, "Aren't they adorable?"

"Are you going to buy one?" I ask.

"No," she smiles. "Not yet. I want one for Jack, but Tennie says he doesn't want a dog around the house yet." She giggles. "He says it's bad enough around there with three children." She laughs to herself, as if there were some kind of private joke behind her statement.

"Now then," I say. "May I treat you to a breakfast at the establishment of culinary delight?"

"Oh, Bill," she begins, because she always protests at my invitation. "You shouldn't."

"But I want to," I protest, and eventually she gives in.

"Let me do my shopping first," she says, and declares her independence by going off to shop from a butcher whom I know to be inferior to the butcher I patronize, but she is impervious to my arguments. ("Well, I've never had a bad cut of meat from him," she says, ignoring entirely the matter of price and value.) "I'll meet you here when I'm done."

Then I go off to do my shopping, mostly for apples and hamburger (I am trying to save money on food because, to tell the truth, matters have become just a little tight in the financial budgetary department) and the occasional bit of baked goods from one of the farm wives. Then I wait for her to finish her purchases, and when she comes toward me I take the heavy basket from her arm ("Thank you—whew, that's *heavy*") and we go into the adjoining canteen for a late Saturday breakfast. My stomach is already growling because it is nearly 10 a.m. The farmers have been here for over four hours already, and their sons and daughters are already buying hot dogs and hamburgers as if it were noon.

The canteen is a comfortable place. It's small, of course, and we must perch up on stools like truck-drivers, and there are no menus and the crockery and utensils are strictly utilitarian and unmatched. But the food is market food: untainted, healthy, plentiful, and plainly cooked. Usually we have bacon and eggs. The bacon strips come still with the rinds on, and you have to strip the rind away carefully if you are to get the full value of the meat. Corrie always asks me if, please, she may have a doughnut—as if I were her father. "Of course," I say, although I warn her of the consequences of doughnuts on good feminine figures. She laughs and says that this once she'll splurge and take a chance. She finishes her meal with a coffee and a cigarette, and says, "Thank you, Bill."

But when we were walking home last Saturday we had a strange sort of conversation. She said to me: "You know that fellow who works at my butcher's stall? That big dark one?"

I have to confess that I have not noticed the fellow. "What about him?" I say.

"Oh, nothing. I just wondered if you had noticed him." She looks strangely troubled and yet looks as if she *liked* being troubled.

"Now, now," I say. "You can't bring up a subject like that and then let it drop."

"Oh," she says. Then: "Well, he told me this morning that I looked like a gypsy. He said he had a picture at home of somebody who looked just like me."

I wondered to myself just what kind of a picture he might have.

I admitted to her that she did look rather more gypsy-like than anyone I had seen around Fredericton. "Your hair," I said, "is very long—and your eyes are very big."

"Yes," she agreed. "I suppose that's it. Still, he keeps *looking* at me."

"How do you mean?"

"You know. He just looks at me."

"Well," I say, "I wouldn't worry about it."

"Oh I don't," she says. "He's probably just in love with me or something like that." She laughs it off.

"You can always change your butcher," I tell her, but she repeats her argument that he has never given her a "bad cut of meat".

"You needn't spend any more time—or money—at that stall than is necessary."

"I suppose you're right," she laughed.

"Does he know you're married?"

"Yes," she said. "You know, today he said to me — 'And what will it be for you today Mrs. . . . ?' He left it for me to fill in my name."

"And did you?"

"I'm afraid I did. But he knew I was married."

"Well, I wouldn't worry about it if I were you. This isn't the States, after all."

She agreed with me. I asked her if Tennie would mind, and she said that she didn't know, but she had no intention whatever of telling him. And I wasn't to, either. I said I considered myself sworn to secrecy.

Then we were back at our house, and I gave her her basket and she went in. I came into my side of the house and opened a can of Campbell's Beef'n'Noodle Soup, which was my lunch.

But I think she was right to be wary of a butcher. It is difficult to explain, of course, but a man is often marked by his occupation. Indeed, it might even be said that I am marked by mine, although less and less each day, I think, as I have moved steadily away from the chalk and blackboards of the classroom. But a butcher now. A butcher is dangerous. He deals in meat, and therefore with man's most carnivorous instincts, and he doesn't work with the meat in all its social amenities, either, like a cook. The meat is the animal. The animal must be killed in the bare room full of sawdust. The blood must be drained away. The hide must be stripped off, and the carcass prepared for the butchery block, and the animal must then be chopped up for consumption. And once you begin to kill — as Adam had to, once he was evicted from the Garden of Eden — then it is difficult to stop killing. Thus we have wars, and Vegetarianism is no defence.

Meat, death, mortality, sex. It is a frightening progression, and Corrie is wise to be frightened of it.

Yet another fluffy snowstorm has buried the stately city of Fredericton.

I was called from my first nervous cup of morning coffee by the ringing of the telephone. The ringing set my nerves on edge and upset my stomach, which still seems to be of the opinion that I must rise to go to work, and it rebels, as it has so often before. I suppose that this was about 10 a.m.

"Is that you, Bill?" she said, and I said, because I was in no mood to be charming, "There's no one else who lives here."

Corrie said: "Bill, I'm sorry, but I have to go to the airport. Will you drive me?"

The idea struck crazily across my mind that she and Tennie had decided to get a divorce. And perhaps there was some reason for the idea because, almost without being aware of it, I had become aware that she and Tennie had furious arguments. If I could not hear the exact words which were sometimes spoken in anger and replied to in fury, none the less I could sometimes hear the movement of the argument: upstairs, downstairs, and in my lady's chamber. It has struck me that they seem to argue with no thought of the effect on the children. Of course, the children argue as well — although more haphazardly — and *their* arguments seem to be restricted to the area of the bumbling television set.

But Corrie explained. "Bill, my mother has just died, and I have to fly home."

I must have hesitated for a moment or two, because she said: "Bill, can you drive a car?"

"Of course I can drive a car," I said. "When do you want to go?"

"There's a plane leaving for Boston in an hour. I can't get hold of Tennie," she explained. "He's in a seminar or something."

It occurred to me that Tennie was probably drinking coffee in the Faculty Club.

"What about the children?" I asked.

"Alisha is going to stay with a friend—Mary Jane Cronke—and I'm taking the boys." (How quickly children make friends.)

"Why not leave the boys here?"

"Tennie couldn't look after them."

"I could look after them," I volunteered.

She paused for just a moment. "I thought about that—but it wouldn't be a good idea, Bill. I can't leave just one—they get so damned jealous, and . . . no, no, it just wouldn't work."

I suppose that then I was thinking about the expense—the incredible cost of the airfare to transport Corrie and her two boys down to the States. I had forgotten just how much more a college professor is paid than a lowly high-school teacher.

Perhaps she guessed what I was thinking. "I think we can afford it, Bill," she said gently.

"Are you ready to go?"

"Yes. I've been getting ready while trying to call Tennie. But Bill—look, I can call a taxi."

"No, no. I'll take you."

I put on my coat, gloves, and overshoes, and got an old shovel out of the basement. (The Garretts had forgotten it and had never come to reclaim it.) Tennie never thought to carry a shovel in his VW bus, having some sort of faith in its advertised ability to keep going. Despite the law, he never bothered to get snow tires for it either, arguing that they never drove much of anyplace in the winter anyway. Nor did he ever have it washed. I had noticed that it was already rusting out.

When we got into the microbus I asked Corrie how to put the damn thing into reverse, and she said she didn't know. "I never learned how to drive," she apologized.

Her nose was red and shiny. She had a slight cold, and

she had been crying. Robert and Jack were jumping up and down in the back of the bus, making a racket (presumably Tennie permitted them this liberty), and I had to tell them to calm down.

Corrie pointed to the little gear diagram on the dashboard of the VW, and I figured it out and finally got the car into reverse. You had to jam down on the gearshift before you could move it into the reverse position. With a certain amount of jumping and bucking and slipping in the new snow, I got the car pointed out the Lincoln Road toward the Fredericton Airport.

Corrie was huddled down into her coat, and I wanted to tell her to go ahead and cry if she wanted to—but that, probably, would not have been the thing to say.

I drove carefully on the way to the airport, mindful of the perils of the new snow and the unfamiliar car, wary of the idiocy of the other drivers and my own rusty driving skills. Corrie said: "For the first time in my life I feel like a grown-up."

It had apparently taken her mother's death for her to realize that she herself had stopped "growing up". She was "grown". She had evidently always thought of herself as a child reaching for the future, and now that future was here.

And if this were true, where did that put me? My father died when I was seven, or one, look at it how you will. Indeed, by this kind of reasoning, how much older than Corrie was I? The sheer chronological years are relatively unimportant, I would assume. When I was around thirty, Corrie had been a mere eighteen, taking off her clothes for the pleasure of Tennie-the-Lifeguard back at the children's camp in Michigan. Writhing in sexual passion on the sandy soil beneath the pine trees while I was holding order in some dusty classroom. What is the role of sexual awakening upon one's *real* age?

But I said the usual things: "Is one of your brothers looking after the arrangements?" I avoided the word "funeral".

"Oh yes," she said, with an unexpected bitterness. "The arrangements will be looked after and looked after and looked *after*. Henry will do one thing and George will argue with him. If Henry picks out the undertaker, George will disagree. We'll have arguments over every meal," she said, glumly.

"What about your father?"

"He's retired," she said. "He does whatever the boys tell him to. George manages an insurance firm, and Henry," she said with a note of apology and guilt in her voice, "Henry works for the Department of Defense."

"Oh."

I carried their bags into the terminal and saw them checked through the Air Canada counter. I looked after Jack and Robert while Corrie went to the ladies' room, and then we all had time for a quick cup of hot chocolate. In fact, we had plenty of time, because when we went back to the waiting-room to watch for the plane, it was announced that the plane would be forty-five minutes late, due to last night's storm. It was all right, Corrie said. They had a four-hour layover in Boston.

"Is there anything—anything at all—that you need?" I said.

"No, I don't think so," she said. "I left a long note for Tennie." I should have expected that.

We sat quietly and waited for the plane. Once or twice it was necessary for me to explain to the boys that they oughtn't to run around the waiting-room. I understood their impatience, but a waiting-room was no place to play tag. Corrie said that she hoped they would be tired enough to sleep on the flight.

Corrie was just wondering if perhaps she oughtn't to try one more time to reach Tennie at the University when the plane suddenly appeared and flashed down the runway.

"Was your mother's death unexpected?" I asked.

"Yes and no. Mother was getting old — but she was one of those women who are never sick a day in their lives. Like me," she added.

The Viscount's screaming engines were cut and it was suddenly very silent. The boarding steps were lowered, and the few passengers emerged into the blowing snow. The commissionaire opened the gate for the boarding passengers who were shuffling forward.

"I don't believe the flight will be crowded," I said.

"No, I don't think so." Corrie smoothed her hair and put on her fur cap. "How's my lipstick, Bill?"

"It looks extremely nice," I said.

"Well, then . . . " She was looking at me. "Boys," she said without looking around, "thank Mr. Boyd for bringing us out."

"Thank you, Mr. Boyd," the boys announced, nearly in unison. They were pleased with their trick and laughed. I thought that Jack was getting just a little old for that kind of behaviour. But they were anticipating the flight and were in a holiday mood. They had never been on a plane before.

"And thank you, Bill," she said again.

"I was pleased to be able to help," I said.

They went out, ducking into the wind which was whipping down the runway. The stewardess at the top of the steps had a hand cupped over her ear to keep it warm. At the top of the boarding steps Corrie turned to wave to me, and I waved in return.

When I got back I parked Tennie's car carefully in its ruts — because he had never taken the time to shovel out his driveway properly, of course — and then I took my shovel out of the back of the car and began to clear the snow (which was falling heavily again) from the walks which led from our respective doors to the sidewalk. By now the snow is piled up four or five feet high on either side of the walk, and I have noticed that when Corrie and I have returned from one of our sojourns in town, we part at the front walk and then are unable to get a glimpse of one another until we reach our porches.

But that evening Tennie came over to thank me for "ferrying" his wife to the airport. I invited him in, of course, and he was pleased to accept. He was in a light-hearted mood (almost "beside himself"), and seemed to want to tease me.

That was perfectly understandable, of course. He was suddenly set free of the habitual patterns of his life, and this sudden freedom can easily take the form of light-headed enjoyment – until the sense of loneliness sets in. He sat down in my living-room and drank coffee with me – but he had a difficult time keeping his seat. He kept standing up to walk around and look out the window, thrusting his hands in his pockets – for all the world like a man who is waiting for the weather to clear so that he can get outside. Now, mind you, the weather was still a steadily falling snow, but that would be no bar to activity. It was simply that Tennie didn't know what to do with himself. He was at loose ends, and his conversation reflected it.

He said: "I think I'll take in a movie at the Gaiety tonight."

"What's playing?" I asked.

Then he said: "I haven't any idea," but he was no longer thinking about the movie at all. He was rushing away on a new thought.

"How are the mortgage rates these days?" he said.

I replied that as far as I knew – according to the papers – they were still over 9 per cent and showed no indication of dropping. I did not mention the mortgage rate on my house. But I wondered why he was suddenly interested in houses.

He turned to grin at me. "Oh," he laughed, "I'm just

playing a game with myself — thinking about the real estate market and all that."

"Are you planning to buy a house?"

"Not right now," he laughed. "I couldn't raise the down payment on a henhouse right now."

He could, of course. He is incredibly well-paid, as I know from Corrie. But it would probably not be a wise investment at the present time.

"Do you find it expensive to heat the place?"

"This place?" I said.

"Yes."

"I don't know yet," I told him. "We'll have to see how the winter goes. So far it's not bad. We'll have to see."

I surmised that he was wondering about the possibility of a new furnace.

"Is your side warm enough?"

"Oh, sure, sure."

"Yes," I agreed. "So far it doesn't seem to be a difficult house to heat."

"I've been down to the CMHC office to look at small-house plans," he confessed.

"The trouble with building now," I pointed out, "is the high cost of land. It raises your assessment to an artificially high figure because the cost of land increases the value of the property well beyond the actual value of the house — so you're taxed for more than you actually have. It's better to buy an older house."

"There aren't many available," he said.

"That's true," I said. "And I'll bet that the house plans available under the CMHC plan aren't much."

"They're utilitarian," he said, but did not wish to commit himself further. "It's just a game with me," he repeated. "I like to go through the motions of buying a house without actually doing it, just for the practice."

"Well," I said, "inasmuch as you haven't a lease here you ought to be able to move quickly if you have a mind to."

"Oh," he replied quickly. "I wasn't hinting at anything like that. It's only a game."

"So you say." I wondered to myself how seriously he was playing the game, but a few inquiries led me to believe that he hadn't investigated very far. He did not even know, for example, that banks do not lend mortgage money here. I had to explain to him about the various trust companies — as well as the fact that if he bought a "country place" he would have to pay higher mortgage rates and higher insurance costs. Rural romanticism is expensive these days. He wasn't really in the game at all.

"I think I'll go see a movie," he said again.

"Without knowing what's *on*?" I said.

"Well, what *else* is there to do?"

Frankly, I was amazed at the way he had time to waste. It seemed to me that he ought to have been preparing his lectures or marking papers, or at least waiting for Corrie to call.

I asked him if Corrie was going to call and he said he didn't know. "Well, perhaps she'll call here if you're not in, and I'll take a message," I said.

"Thanks," he said.

Therefore I sat home that evening, waiting for their phone to ring, and then mine. Theirs rang once, but not long enough to have been a long-distance call. Mine did not ring at all.

AN ALIEN'S GUIDE TO SURVIVAL. (Continued)

And if we accept the Principle of *Rejection* as the necessary *Premise* for the survival of Mankind, then it follows that we must not be timid about its use or its effects. Thus, we must not only reject the industrial economy and its poisonous factories, but we must also reject the cash-economy itself, which is the result of industrialization.

One need only look at the present situation. Because we have become a "Cash-Economy" we have "impoverished" hundreds and thousands of farmers. The small farm, we are told, is no longer "economically viable". *However*, it is clear that the farmer can easily grow sufficient food to *feed his family*, although he cannot *turn a profit*. That is, he cannot sell the surplus in order to buy the so-called "necessities" of life, such as automobiles. But I would argue that these are *false* necessities, and that the entire "cash-economy" is nothing more than a trumped-up system, devised by, and in aid of, commercial enterprise. Furthermore, the commercial economy has led us to accept *cities* as representing the only way of life. Thus we are forever attempting to devise means to "improve our cities", when in fact we ought to abandon them to rot. (Rotting, of course, is a perfectly *natural* thing.)

We must return to the rural life once again because, to put it simply, the farm provides man with his natural necessities: food, shelter, and fuel. And a man need not attempt to "make a profit", because the only *purpose* of the farm is to feed the man and his family, and provide for their necessities. Thus a man will raise the crops necessary for his table and necessary for feeding his stock. He will grow and cut the wood necessary to build and heat his dwelling-place. Man will become *self-sufficient*, and his happiness and dignity will be increased thereby.

And if it should be argued that such a plan, however necessary, would result in a somewhat primitive mode of life, then I would say: *so be it*. But I would argue further that a little *ingenuity* would not merely ensure man's survival, but would make it quite comfortable.

For example, one of the curses of the Maritime region in general and New Brunswick in particular has been the *imposed* necessity of trade beyond its borders. The natural economy of New Brunswick has been turned over to the commercial myth, and thus we sell our products and resources both to the United States and to Upper Canada in return for cash, and then spend our cash to buy back their material goods. We lose both ways. Our resources go out, and the resulting cash goes out as well, resulting in a twofold drain on the natural economy of the province. Because we have developed a false economy whereby we must have *cash* to buy automobiles, we have sold New Brunswick's birthright for the *cost of a car,* the money for which returns to Ontario. (I am not here suggesting—at least for the present—that a separation of New Brunswick from the confederation known as Canada might be necessary.)

But suppose we developed an internal economy, directed toward the natural life of New Brunswick. Suppose we rejected the principle of "foreign trade" altogether. ("Foreign trade" is, at any rate, a nineteenth-century doctrine of British imperialism, perhaps necessary for the maintenance of nineteenth-century Britain, but not necessarily a pattern to be followed elsewhere, *in this time, in this place.*) Suppose we decided to develop an economy suited to the happiness of New Brunswick, and gave up trying to emulate the Joneses of Ontario and the United States.

We would need a mode of transport. We have waterways which could easily be utilized (the Saint John River and the Miramichi), and it would be relatively easy to revitalize the decaying railway system. Indeed, it is true that within its borders New Brunswick has sufficient iron deposits to produce all the steel necessary for its uses. Railways could be built. (The automobile would be abandoned altogether. It is not particularly suited to the New Brunswick climate anyway.)

Certainly New Brunswick is perfectly capable of growing sufficient food to feed its population, and indeed, sufficient to enable the farmer to trade with the townsman in return for certain crafts. Thus a carpenter could trade his work for food; thus the tailor could provide the clothes necessary for the farmer in return for a certain allotment of food.

Now, *if* it should be necessary (because all men are ambitious) that one man might find himself unfairly done-by by this system, we could introduce some elementary form of goods exchange, which might even be represented by a kind of *script*. This, the best tailor would soon acquire a reputation for his good work, and would receive a surplus of food orders. He would not need all the food he would receive, and would therefore bargain with the local carpenter to build him a house. I admit that *script* would make this much more efficient.

But we should not trade beyond our borders. Foreign trade puts one at the mercy of foreign governments and must be avoided even before foreign treaties.

But I must stress this matter of ingenuity. The fact is that the cash-economy system has made us all short-sighted. We are afraid to set forth upon any enterprise which might make us happier because the system is so overwhelming and complex that it frightens us. We are so much at the whims of international economy that we are afraid to *make our way in a small way*.

For example, it is clear that New Brunswick could easily develop a unique tourist economy simply by a little thought. We could set up immense camps throughout the province (they would not destroy the ecology) which would be supervised by the government, and run trains to them. Hundreds of thousands of American tourists could be brought in in the summer and they would be gone before winter. We could provide them with clean air and clean water and, that most precious commodity of all: silence. (Consider the vastness of central New Brunswick; consider how silent it must be.) There would be no need to depend upon the government in Ottawa for funds, or for the economy of Upper Canada for goods. We would be our own masters.

Even further. I am constantly struck by the lack of imagination which is *everywhere evident*, the lack of *courage*. For example, it happens that I am well enough off (due to foresight, economy, and planning), but if it were necessary for me to make a living in Fredericton, I assure you that I could do it quite easily.

Indeed, because this is a university town, the first thing I would do would be to open some kind of used-book service. I might begin with a cart of used books (I have enough of my own to start, although I would be loath to part with them, for they are old friends), which I would trundle to the market on Saturdays and, in fine summer weather, take down on the Green by the cathedral and the art gallery. I could sell sufficient books to keep me in food.

Or again, one might consider expanding the notion somewhat. If it is true that Fredericton is too small a city to support a bookshop which is *nothing but a bookshop*, then I would diversify my interests. Fredericton needs a bookshop, but it also needs a shop which sells fine spices and good cheeses. Corrie has often complained to me that she cannot find the most usual of interesting cheeses. (She has a taste for Limburger.) Therefore my shop would have one wall of books, and a counter along the other wall full of spices and cheeses. Indeed, much the same clientele would be served by both.

And if I wished to get rich, I would expand my shop to make it into a coffee-house – perhaps a room at the back. For it is true that there is nowhere in Fredericton where one may enjoy the quiet amenities of life – good conversation, good coffee, and a homely "treat". I would serve a "setting" of a cup of coffee (with whipped cream), a slice of good Taymouth cheese (locally available), and a McIntosh apple (from Keswick Ridge), all for 25¢. I would make my fortune.

One day last week I happened to interrupt my labours to go down to the basement, where I fancied I heard the old furnace making strange noises. I had not bothered to turn on the lights because there was sufficient light from the little windows for my purposes. Besides, I intended merely to listen and to sniff for any possible danger. I was using other senses than the much over-worked visual one.

Then as I stood there in the damp shadow of the old furnace, listening to the mutter of its heat, I saw Corrie descend into her side of the basement. She was wearing her housecoat and slippers. Her arms were laden with a load of children's underwear, destined for the washer, and consequently she could not turn on the lights either.

You ought to know that the basement can be illuminated by a switch in either stairway which descends to the basement. I have often found it necessary to turn out the lights after Tennie or one of the children have been to the basement to begin some venture which they have shortly abandoned.

I stood there in the shadow of the old furnace and watched Corrie shove the children's underwear into her washing machine. I was surprised to notice how silent she was. Somehow I had expected her to be humming—or at least talking to herself. But she was lost *in herself*, as the saying goes, and made no sound whatever save those of her activity.

When I cleared my throat to warn her of my presence, she screamed.

"It's just me," I explained quickly. There was no one else in the house.

"Oh, Bill, you scared me half to death." She tried to catch her breath. "What in the world are you doing down here in the dark?"

I explained that I had come down to check the furnace.

"Is it burning too much oil?" she inquired.

"Not too much," I said, pleased with her concern. "I'm very sorry I frightened you."

"Oh," she laughed. "I wasn't really frightened. I mean, I was just scared witless there for a second. It's just that I always think there is someone hiding in the shadows." She was ashamed to confess her fear to me. "I suppose I *was* frightened, wasn't I?"

"Of course you were. It's perfectly understandable."

"It's just that—you know how it is in the States. You never know *who* you'll find in your basement. There's at least one mass-murderer or sex maniac in every neighbourhood. Or at least it seems that way."

"Yes," I said.

"There was one in mine," she said. "A housewife was found stabbed to death. I was just a little girl. They never knew who did it. In broad daylight. My mother never explained," she laughed. "Maybe it was her husband. And," she added, "it was a very *good* neighbourhood."

"Yes," I said. "That's one reason we're all here."

"It's a relief to be able to walk across the street to the store after dark, at least," she said.

Therefore I now find myself worried about Corrie. She has descended into the cockpit of democracy which the United States has become, and I do not even know where she has gone—I do not know her "home town" any more than she knows that I have none. I could ask Tennie where she is, of course, but I am ashamed.

Because there is nothing which incites a feeling of—could one dare call it adoration?—more quickly than a shared, mutual fear.

I too am afraid of shadows. I am afraid of shadows because someone could be hiding in the shadows, ready to leap out and drag me into the alleys of the underworld, where a profitable knife would make short work of me.

Yet it was an American who gave the popular definition of courage. I am thinking of Franklin Delano Roosevelt, who said that "we have nothing to fear but fear itself." An American knows about that, certainly. And perhaps it is worth remembering that even Roosevelt found it necessary to escape from the maelstrom of rampant democracy (for which he was largely responsible!) to Campobello Island, New Brunswick. He wanted the best of both worlds. I do not blame him. Like the early settlers of New Brunswick, he knew that Democracy was not a form of government to be trusted for long. To believe in a Democracy you must fool yourself that man is *naturally good*, and that, of course, is nothing more than a *delusion*.

Five

"Tut-tut" one says. "Tut-tut."

No, one does *not* say tut-tut. Rather, I hear my mother saying "tut-tut", saying it, moreover, while she is standing in the centre of our regularly scoured, sweet-smelling, pink-decorated, feminine bathroom in the apartment above the dime-store. She says "tut-tut" and shoves some clothes deeper into the laundry-hamper. I do not know what has caused her to say "tut-tut" over the laundry, and I do not *wish* to know, so I ignore the problem. She, on her part, is putting away the problem by saying "tut-tut". She means to put the problem away without discussion. It is not worthy of discussion in her opinion, or perhaps it is a matter *not to be discussed,* and I am therefore spared the uncomfortable confrontation, although I am left with a faint feeling of guilt.

One must learn to face up to things.

The bathroom was newly decorated in pink, as I recall, and Mother was proud of it. It marked our achievement of respectability. The wall by the tub had been tiled in pink, and pink towels had been acquired for guest occasions, which came seldom enough, although Mother often entertained the ladies from her church circle. A pink chenille toilet-seat cover appeared, so that when the toilet-seat was dropped, there was no longer a resounding bang which echoed through the house to announce one's activity to the ladies who paused only briefly over their teacups. I could return to my room in silence, unheard and unnoticed.

But this little affair will not be put aside by a "tut-tut".

The invitation was casual enough. One might say in fact that it was *deceptively casual.* Tennie telephoned to say that there were "a few people dropping by for a drink" that evening, and would I care to join them?

I said that it was very good of him to think of me. Would Corrie be back?

No, he said. He did not "believe" that Corrie would be back until next week.

"And the dress?" I inquired casually. He misunderstood me.

"The address?" he asked incredulously.

I explained. "What should I wear?"

"Oh hell, Bill, whatever you feel like. It's all pretty casual. Lots of people, talk, drink – that sort of thing – OK?"

Indeed: OK. I agreed to attend. I wore my blue suit and a white shirt (with a red plaid tie) and looked for all the world like a schoolteacher or a Baptist minister. I am aware of these things. When I entered I looked so strange – among *that* gathering – that I nearly stopped conversation.

I knocked and was admitted by a fat man about Tennie's age. Tennie craned his neck around the corner from the kitchen and called out, "Hi, Bill." And then I turned my attention toward the living-room and saw only a collection of moon-like faces turned toward me.

Tennie had turned out all the lights and the house was "lit" entirely by candles. My first thought was: my eyes will adjust to this in a moment. My second thought was: lighting by candles is a very risky business indeed, and it's a good thing I have fire insurance. The curse of a duplex is that one is at the mercy of one's neighbours. My third thought was: what a collection of people! Hell must be like this.

They were dressed in every kind of attire imaginable. For example, the fat fellow who admitted me was wearing khaki trousers, a nondescript sweater, and dirty old tennis-shoes. But he was now standing by a slender, elegant young woman in a long shimmering green gown. Diamonds—or rhinestones—sparkled from her neck and wrist. She had long, raven-black hair; her eyes were made up to emphasize their darkness, her white skin. She eyed me coolly and turned back into the gathering.

There *was* a large crowd there. Tennie had told me "9 p.m.", and it was 9.15, but the party had the air of having begun earlier.

The fat fellow said: "You must be the cow-hand."

"The cow-hand?"

"Ah . . . Mr. *Boyd*," he said.

So they had been spreading my name about in banter. It is a very tired joke, and this inept soul could not even get the joke straight.

"I am William Boyd," I said.

"We've been out skiing," he said. "Or maybe I ought to say that we've been out drinking in the woods." He gave a short little laugh. A glance at his eyes confirmed the truth of his statement. I imagined them standing in the snow, raising their glasses to one another as in a whiskey ad. He stuck out his puffy hand toward me.

"I'm Morley," he said.

"How do you do," I said.

"The drinks are this way," he said, and led me into the dining-room. There I discovered that Tennie had shoved the dining-room table up against the wall under a window, and on it there was an array of liquor bottles. Obviously they were well into the bottles. Some were nearly full (the rum, for instance), but others — the gin and scotch — were nearly empty. I was informed that I could help myself, and Mr. Morley returned to the elegant young woman of the rhinestones.

I have always considered myself impervious to insult. I have a certain number of years of experience for one thing, and if one can withstand the sniggering mockeries of a high-school pupil, one can withstand nearly anything. Again, I have always endeavoured to think things through. To know where one stands is to be prepared for challenges.

Tennie came stomping toward me, his smile flashing from his height as he ducked through the door. The "ducking" of his head was an affectation; it was not really necessary. His hand was clasped around a glass of whiskey in which the ice-cubes rattled. He was wearing a tuxedo, I noticed, complete with a ruffled-front shirt.

"Have you got yourself a drink? There's more ice in the kitchen."

"You didn't tell me it was a costume party."

"What? Oh, well — it just sort of *happened*," he laughed. "We kind of *created* it as we went along."

He looked at his feet, and my glance inevitably followed his. He tugged at his trousers to reveal his ankles. He was wearing ski-boots.

"They're damned comfortable," he said. "Except to walk in, of course. Help yourself to a drink."

He clomped back to the kitchen.

The house, I perceived, was full of Tennie's academic and "arty" friends. Indeed, on all sides there was the flutter of arrogantly erudite conversation, ponderous with the certainty of heavy knowledge. It was the sort of conversation which shoves wit aside with its own confidence. I wondered if Corrie were comfortable among these people or their kind—or if perhaps Tennie had waited until she was out of town to invite them in. As far as I knew, this was Tennie's first party.

The truth is that I detest parties. Artificial, drink-induced jollity depresses me. Is this what man is reduced to?

I went over to the table where the bottles were, found a glass, put in a few drops of rye whiskey, and added a good deal of water.

Tennie waded toward me, pulling on the hand of a creature who was squeaking something over her shoulder in the direction of the kitchen.

"Bill," he said. "This is Mary."

"Marie," she said automatically, and looked at me with a doubtful eye—although what right she had to be doubtful I do not know. She was a square little woman. Her black party-dress (with full sleeves) was quite short; her bosom was quite large. The dress fell from this protuberance to her faintly quivering thighs, and gave her the look of a gauzy black funeral package with legs.

Tennie tried again. "This is Miss Something-or-Other." It sounded like "Pettipants", but surely that was not her name. She had a round, large jaw, a pug nose, and heavily made-up eyes. She wore a flagrant pink lipstick. Her head was a mass of black curls. She put her hand to her head and moved the mass a few points in a clockwise direction. Thus I knew she was wearing a wig.

"How do you do," I said. "I'm William Boyd."

"You're the landlord," she announced.

"That's right," I said. "And you?"

"I teach," she said flatly.

"Ah," I said. "And what do you teach?"

"Whatever I'm paid to," she said.

"Well, would you like me to get you a drink?"

"I've got one," she said. It was evident that it was not her first.

"Well," I said, striving for conversation. "What do you get paid to teach?"

"Nothing that would interest you," she said. "You see that man over there?" She gestured toward a tall fellow who looked like a western singing-star.

"Yes."

"He's a famous Canadian poet," she said. "But you wouldn't know about that, would you?" She took a gulp from her glass and said, "Never mind. Neither do the Canadians."

"Is he a good poet?"

"I don't know," she said. "I teach sociology."

She asked me if I had a cigarette. I said that I did not, and explained that I do not smoke. She wandered off and I thought that I would be left alone, but in a few moments she was back, waving her cigarette at me.

"You know," she said, blowing smoke around our heads, "you were invited for me."

"Oh," I said. "How is that?"

"I think someone with a feeble sense of humour is playing matchmaker," she said. "But I do not intend to be rolled into anyone's bed on a cart," she said.

To keep my composure *at that* it was necessary for me to take a large drink of my whiskey. I had intended to nurse the drink for a decent interval and then express my regrets and leave, but on this occasion I very nearly drained it off at a gulp.

More people seemed to be arriving. There was a blast of

cold air as they entered, a stamping of feet, and lumps of snow melted into puddles of water on the floor of the entrance-way. People ascended and descended the stairs. Coats were trundled up. Young women came down looking around to be noticed, laughing self-consciously. Men made their burrowing way to the table of bottles with exaggerated gusto.

"Well, you're no great catch yourself," she said.

"Thank you," I said.

"You're welcome," she said.

I thought that perhaps I was bony and lank, but at least I was not fat.

"I've got to go to the john," she announced.

"You're excused," I said, and she waddled off to find the potty.

By this time, of course, the house was crowded. It was so crowded that one might say that we were smoking one another's cigarettes. It was decidedly uncomfortable for a non-smoker, and my eyes were smarting. I found myself pressed back against the living-room wall by a crush of dark, strange bodies, and I thought of all the space and privacy available on the other side of the house—and longed for it.

Tennie seemed to be the only person able to move with any ease—possibly because he was taller than anyone else and could therefore see over the crowd to see where he was going—but probably because he was wearing those ski-boots. They served as bludgeons down there in the dark.

"Have you got a drink, Bill?"

"Yes I have. Thank you."

"Bill, this is Frank Morley." He put a hand on the elbow of Morley, who was standing, embarrassed, beside him.

"We've met," I said.

"Bill is an American," he said, referring to me. Then, turning his attention away from Morley to me, he said:

"They're going to deport us, you know. All of us."

"Oh, I don't think anything like that will happen," began Morley. "It's merely a matter of . . . "

"Frank has just left his wife," said Tennie. "He's living at the Windsor Hotel with all the other men who have left their wives."

"I don't believe there are any others there," began Morley.

"Is your wife here?" I said.

"Good Lord, I hope not!" said Morley, looking around.

"That would be shocking, wouldn't it?" said Tennie.

"Bad taste," said Morley, and giggled.

It was now nearly impossible to pick out an individual face in the crowd. By this I mean that the room had become so crowded that the very accumulation of bodies and the *resultant mass* had crowded out the light. Most of the candles were set on end tables, etc. Yes, and at least one woman had screeched that she had been burned — which she hadn't, and no one paid much attention to her — although one academic *had* burned a hole in the sleeve of his coat. He cursed with a certain low-minded repetition. It was now necessary to move as some laboratory animal might (an animal being used to predict the effect of over-crowding upon the social organism), by the senses of touch and smell. Strangers were crushed up against strangers. If one noticed a whiff of perfume in the smoky air, then there was a woman near by. Conversation, of course, had virtually ceased, and mere comments were being shouted at people.

"What's that?"

"I said: 'How's *that* for stupid.'"

"Oh. Yes, yes. You're right, of course."

I started to make my way toward the door, believing that I would be able to escape without being noticed. But as I manoeuvred my way around a cluster of vehement people who were discussing (foolishly, I thought) the so-called "student rebellion", I found myself between Tennie and the elegant young woman in rhinestones.

She was much younger than I had thought. She could not have been more than twenty years old, and my first reaction was that it must be the practice for academics to marry young wives — as Tennie had done. But that wasn't it at all.

Tennie was looking earnestly at the girl and saying, "Now — if you had the chance to be *any*where you wanted to be *right now*, where would you be?"

She was looking fondly at him, and was saying, "I think I'd like to be right here with . . . " when Tennie noticed me.

"Ah," he said with remarkable aplomb. "It's our landlord, Bill Boyd. Bill Boyd, this is Miss Spenser."

"How do you do," I said. "I was just . . . "

"Miss Spenser was just telling me where she would like to go on holiday." A meaningful glance passed between them.

"Oh," she said quickly. "I think I'd like to go to Ireland. Yes. Ireland would be nice."

I said: "Ireland is a Papist country, and while Papists are to be forgiven their ignorance, they ought not be indulged in it. The same might be said of children," I added, "or students."

"Bill," said Tennie quickly. "How about having another drink?"

"Why not?" I said, and Tennie looked surprised.

I turned to get one and asked Miss Spenser if perhaps she was Catholic.

"No," she said.

"Then I won't have to apologize for the rudeness of my opinion, will I?"

She was open-mouthed. I edged myself away, and as I made my way into the dining-room I could see Tennie's head, bent close to Miss Spenser's ear.

It is a common attitude, you see, to assume that if one holds an "unfashionable" idea, one is therefore crazy. It saves thinking about the idea. And of course one of the current fashions is to be "tolerant" about Roman Catholicism. The attitude of tolerance saves one the trouble of thought. That is, one is supposed to cast a wry (and dishonest) smile towards the doctrinaire stupidities of the Roman Catholic Church which are crowding out the world. But there comes a time when *tolerance* becomes *dishonesty*, and *dishonesty* abets an *evil*. That God should have told the Pope that the Pope was to speak for God, and that God would have men and women propagate themselves into starvation for the enrichment of the Church at Rome! Faugh!

Then, as I was edging my way toward the kitchen in search of ice-cubes and water (for both had long since disappeared from the table of drinks, and, in fact, some of the guests were pouring gin into half-empty tonic bottles and then swigging straight from the bottle), I bumped into Morley, who was blocking the doorway.

He was standing in a drunken lump, being harangued by a young man with wild hair and steel-rimmed spectacles — very much like the kind which James Magee used to wear before he gave them up in the faith that the strain would strengthen his eyes. Magee bought his at the dime-store, trying on pair after pair until he got the right ones. It is quite likely that the young man wears his merely to be fashionable.

I said to this Morley: "Are there students here as well as faculty?"

He turned his head slowly to me (the young man did not seem to mind the loss of Morley's "attention") and looked at me in puzzlement, trying to recollect who I was. I repeated my question.

"Sure," he said. "Why not?"

"Miss Spenser?"

"Who?"

"Over there." I pointed.

"Yeah. She's a student." He giggled. "Good-looking little thing, ain't she?"

Miss Spenser, I perceived, was now in deep conversation with the wild-haired young man. He was talking with rapid gestures of his hands in order to express his sincerity, and she was nodding. The hands were to make up the argument, I supposed.

Tennie approached from one side as I did from the other.

The wild-haired young man seemed to be pleading, saying, "No, no, that won't *do it.* There's got to be some kind of *move*ment, some kind of *touch*—like with outer space."

Tennie dropped into their conversation as neatly as a dealt card. "Ecstasy, perhaps?"

"Ecstasy," said Miss Spenser.

"Because," continued the young man, "if there's no *vision—vision*, you understand, then life isn't worth living. You've go to *see inside.*"

"And ecstasy," said Tennie, swaying slightly (I noticed that he was drunk), "is the union of the *inner visions.*" He was visibly pleased with his statement.

The wild-haired young man said: "So we have to use all the means at our disposal to *look inside our heads.* Books once, maybe, but now maybe drugs. If it takes drugs to survive, then we'll use drugs. Huxley," he announced with a note of finality.

"Do you know what I'd do with people who want to take drugs?" I said.

All three of them looked at me *resentfully*. I had intruded upon their *agreement*. The *smugness* of their *toleration*.

"I think that anyone who wants drugs should be allowed to have as many—and as much—as he wants," I said, watching their faces carefully. "Because," I continued, "I think that everyone has the inalienable *right* to commit suicide. But on the other hand, you might as well take a pistol, stick it in your mouth, and pull the trigger. It's a real mind-blowing experience," I said. "But if you want to know what I *really* think," I said, "I think that all of those who use drugs ought to be stood up against a wall and shot. It's neater and more efficient, and better for society in the long run. Don't you agree?"

"Jesus," said Tennie.

"Excuse me while I refill this glass," I said.

Some of the guests had already left the party. At least, there seemed to be more space in the room, and I assumed that those with children had left to see to their baby-sitters. The students were still there, of course, drinking up the free booze. Miss Spenser was sitting on the sofa—and indeed, it was now possible to *see* the sofa. She looked permanently stunned. She was very drunk, and her mouth was a bit crooked on one side, as if she were endeavouring not to drool. The shoulder of her gown was not quite straight—or to her liking—and from time to time she twitched at it.

But in the kitchen an argument raged. Tennie was quite wild with anger, taking little abbreviated paces back and forth like a child who needs to be excused, extending his long arms in exaggerated gestures of despair, nearly spilling the drink which sloshed in its glass in his big hand.

The kitchen itself was a mess. The white plastic garbage pail was overflowing with empty bottles (one broken), orange rind, and some rotten grapes which someone had thrown in. On the counter by the sink there was a collection of empty non-returnable bottles: Canada Dry Tonic, Canada Dry Ginger Ale, Canada Dry Bitter Lemon. Some had fallen over on their sides. A little graveyard of bottles.

Morley was also there, looking on the proceedings with glazed eyes. And the object of Tennie's gestures of despair was the young man with the wild hair and the steel-rimmed glasses, who now looked at Tennie with a certain smugness. He listened to Tennie with his hands stuffed deep into the pockets of his jeans. He was evidently achieving the effect he desired. His name, I discovered (not a little to my surprise), was "Manners".

"Oh, Jesus, Jesus, Manners," Tennie was shouting. "You can't turn an education system *on* and *off* like that."

"Why not?" said Manners, insolently.

"You can't seriously mean that you're going to *deport* all the Americans. Look, you hired us to do a job. You can't just turn us back when the job is finished!"

"Why not?" repeated Manners. "That's what one *does* with itinerant labour."

Morley began to stutter an opinion, but was too drunk to get it out.

"We've learned that from you," continued Manners. "We've learned to take what we want and then to say to hell with the responsibility. It's called the American Foreign Policy," he sniggered.

"Oh—but, Christ, Manners," said Tennie, actually slapping his forehead with his free hand. "I'm against the Vietnam war. You know that. *Every*one knows that. *I'm* not responsible for the U.S. policies."

"Yes you are," insisted Manners. He lit a cigarette very coolly. With his hands on his hips he looked like an advocate who knows he has the jury in his pocket. And why not! Arguing with an immigrant in one's own country, one *always* has the jury in one's pocket, so to speak. Manners continued: "You are as responsible as the Germans were for Nazism."

"But I *left*," howled Tennie.

"Perhaps it was your duty to *stay*," replied Manners, pointing his finger at Tennie. "Perhaps that's why *you* are *responsible*."

I drew Morley aside to ask him what the discussion was all about.

"What?" he said, trying to look at me through his

drunkenness. "She said I was no good, that's all. She said she was *bored* with me."

I endeavoured again to explain to him what it was that I wished to know.

"Oh," he said. "There are too many Americans in Canadian universities," he explained. "Manners is a very bright young man," he added.

Morley's face was very puzzled, as if he had no concern for what he had just said; as if it were all beside the point. He looked at me again as if he had just noticed me. "Say," he began, "have you seen . . . ?" He was unable to complete his sentence because he had forgotten what he began to say. He raised his glass to his lips automatically, and drank. He did not seem to notice that his glass was, in fact, quite empty.

Manners was now pressing on, marking off his points on his fingers. "You have taken over our economy; you have used our resources for *your* industry and polluted *our* country; you have used us as a colony of the United States; and now you are creating an educational system suitable for the needs of the *United States*." He seemed quite satisfied with himself. "Harsh measures are called for," he said, helplessly, as if it were out of his hands.

Tennie squealed. "*I* didn't."

"You're quite right, young fellow," I interrupted. "Americans take over because they are ambitious. They're raised that way. Never have an American for a neighbour."

The expression on Tennie's face was something to behold.

I discovered that Miss Pettipants was right beside me. She had taken off her wig and I was shocked to see that her hair was grey. She announced in a loud, harsh voice: "All Americans are Murderers."

I said to her: "Ah, Miss Pettipants, you're out of the bathroom, I see."

She glared at me scornfully. I thought she looked quite drained.

"Killers," she said.

Of course, one ought not to attempt to discuss anything with a drunk, much less *argue* with one. The only way to a rational conclusion about anything is the mutual acceptance of the *rules of rational argument.* But the drunk, whose vision is distorted to the point that he is no more than a dreaming dog, believes in emotion, and in *emotional vehemence.* Indeed, why else would he decide to get drunk if not to "forget himself"? Large segments of our society seem to have decided that we can *forgive* the drunk's "forgetting himself".

Thus, I should not have entered into the discussion, but I did.

I said to Tennie: "You were speaking of ecstasy as the *union of inner visions.*"

He stared at me, frozen with his hand still raised to make a point—with great sincerity.

"What?"

"I said: 'You were speaking of *ecstasy* as the *union* of *inner visions.*' That's very clever," I said—merely to throw him off balance, I suppose.

"We're not talking about that," he said. "Oh yes you are," I said. "Whether you realize it or not."

"We were talking about the problems of the United States and Canada."

I shook my head. "Not at all—although I will grant you that you *thought* you were talking about that."

Tennie, in his drunkenness, was puzzled.

"What you were in fact talking about *by means of other terms* was the nature of man."

"No."

"Yes," I said.

By this time the pudgy little Miss Pettipants was leaning

her sleepy little head on poor Frank Morley's shoulder. He, in turn, was leaning against the door-jamb, deluding himself that he was merely tired.

"What you were in fact talking about was the Freedom of Man to decide his political destiny, and you chose to do so in terms of an argument which says that members of one nation have the right to do things to members of another. In short, might makes right, depending on the circumstances. But we often talk about one thing when we are really talking about another."

"No," said Tennie.

"Most of all when we least admit it," I said.

The young Manners was leaning back against the counter, lighting yet another cigarette. He looked for some place to throw his spent match, decided (carelessly) upon the trash-basket, and flung the match in that direction. It fell on the floor.

"You simply haven't done your homework," I said to Tennie. "You must *first* start with a definition of the nature of man because, if you begin with a false definition, all the truths which follow will be false. Do you understand that? It is inadmissible evidence, in any case."

"No, dammit," began Tennie.

"Yes," I said. "You believe that man is capable of *ecstasy*, of 'being in touch', I believe."

"I *never* said that," yelped Tennie.

"But," I continued, "you have argued all your points this evening in a vacuum because you have not realized that Man is a Fallen Creature."

And then, while Tennie looked on with astonishment (ah, the ignorant arrogance of the academic, to think that knowledge is a private preserve!), I explained things to him. That if you look upon man as a creature capable of perfection, then it follows that you attempt to construct political systems to *perfect* (verb) *man.* Furthermore, you will idealize the human mating activity into a thing called "love". You will delude yourself that the ecstasy of two people mooning into one another's eyes is the equivalent of metaphysical understanding.

Tennie tried to argue with me, of course, but he was incoherent, unable to muster an analysis of my position.

"Of course you must attack my premises," I told him. "Any thief will tell you that. If a thief begins by saying that theft is honesty, then it follows that thievery is merely an occupation."

"What are you talking about?"

"Big Business," I said.

And I tried earnestly to reveal to him that the only love possible in the universe is the love for Christ, which is UPWARD, because love is not a horizontal activity, between people, but only a yearning for heavenly perfection as represented by *Christ*. And Christ may or may not return it — depending upon His whim.

Tennie attempted to reply to this with a question. He was now lying to himself by means of the "tolerant fallacy". He believed that if he merely "tolerated" me in some sort of amiable, patronizing manner, my arguments would dissipate. But you have only to look around you to know the nature of the world, I said. Indeed, I gestured around me at the kitchen.

Morley and Miss Pettipants had decamped. To what? I wondered.

To flop their flabby bodies on the abandoned bed upstairs?

It is quite possible. Because we are so frightened of the love for God that we prefer to mistake our lust for one another for the love of God, and therefore act accordingly. We thereby imitate the fall of man; we imitate Adam and Eve. We come to know what little we know of God my means of Sin!

Thus, I fell "in love" with Katherine Dobbs, reaching for God. When we borrowed her father's car and took the long ride over to Ripley for a summer evening, I was searching for God. When we got to Ripley we pulled into the Burger Heaven and ate hamburgers (with pickles, mustard, ketchup, fried onions, and tartar sauce) and french fries; drank Cokes. We ate quickly and quietly because both of us were thinking of the coming dark night and the opportunities available to us—parked out there on a lonely country road. When we had finished our meal I would say, "Shall we go?" and she would answer quickly and nervously, "Yes." We left Ripley early so that we would have the long dark time together. So that we would have the time To Fall. We could foresee ourselves being "carried away", fumbling for one another's flesh in gasps and doubts, wanting to *get there* when in fact there was no bottom. We saw ourselves in Flights of Love. Oh, yes, we did. Katherine's yearning groans and her appeals to me to stop, as I always did, were the means by which she maintained the *illusion* of *flight*. But how easy it is to mistake one's *Falling* for *Flight*! We felt ourselves tumbling *free* in our falling, and we thought ourselves flying. We were in ecstasy!

"Ecstasy," I said, "is just another word for dog-like idiocy. I think of it in terms of a dog drooling over his dinner. One might as well be ecstatic about *food*," I said.

Manners was now sitting on the floor of the kitchen, talking to someone or other. The someone-or-other was trying to explain to him that when one is born into a certain context, then there is no *erasing* that context. "As this fellow" (he gestured toward me) "was born an American. He'll never be anything else." Manners laughed at that.

And then, the someone-or-other said, "You are what you are. There's no changing it."

Manners shook his head at the fellow's foolishness.

"I can be whatever I want."

"No you can't," said the fellow. "You think that only

because you are young. But you are still *you*."

I agreed. Manners looked up at me and said, "You're a silly old fart."

I said: "And you, clearly, have blown your mind."

"Why don't you just go away," said Manners. "You're a *bore*. That's what you are. A bore!"

Well, I thought, if you wish to avoid truth by *boredom*, then that's your concern. I started to leave.

But when I went into the by-now-deserted living-room, I came upon the elegant Tennie and the elegant Miss Spenser. Someone had pulled the sofa out into the middle of the floor, and they were sitting on it with their backs to me. They were in all their glory—he in his tuxedo, she in her gown—as if they were posing for an advertisement for some alcoholic mixture which would give them the Good Life. Because I was *behind* them I was chiefly aware of Tennie's regular, handsome profile, and could see only the yearning motions of Miss Spenser's head. She looked down at her lap and then turned a shy glance up at Tennie. He pressed on with his conversation. His long arm—the sleeve with its French cuff, the large, heavy silver cuff-link—was thrown across the back of the sofa in a careless attitude.

I heard Miss Spenser give a vulgar little laugh and make an inquiry of Tennie in very crude terms, although she spoke softly enough. She seemed to be hesitant, but none the less she enjoyed the drunken freedom of her expression. She used a word which sounds messy in the mouth of a woman. Indeed, men who use such words are considered to have "garbage-mouths".

But Tennie seemed to be more flattered than not by her question—perhaps by the question itself, perhaps by the very *intimacy* of the *crudity*. He gave a pleased, raucous laugh in response.

And then he leaned into her ear, and spoke to her like a lover, although the words he spoke referred to a conjugal *secret of Corrie's*! A certain posture; a sexual stance. I wish sincerely that I had not heard those words.

For a multitude of reasons I hope that I am mistaken in what I heard. Perhaps I was.

But Tennie, when he looked up at me—*blushed*. Consider what it takes to make *any* man blush! Consider what it would take to make *Tennie* blush!

He decided to pretend to be a maudlin drunk.

"Hi, Bill, come on in," he said. "Have another drink."

I came into the room and went around the sofa to face them.

"I was just about to leave," I said, "and came in merely to pay my respects to my host."

Tennie laughed scornfully. "Oh, shit, Bill, you're too much, you know that? Too much. Sit down and have a drink. Here," he said to Miss Spenser, "scoot over, sweetie, and make room for the landlord."

"No thanks," I said. "I must be going."

Tennie looked up at me with all the complacency of a Drunk, except that his eyes were too quick, too shrewd.

"You know what your trouble is, Bill," he said, lolling his head around and waving his glass. "You know what your trouble is?"

"No," I said. "Tell me."

"Your trouble is that you're a fool," he said.

"Thank you," I said.

"No, no," he insisted. "You don't understand. There's lots of fools in the world. Your trouble, Bill, is more serious than that."

"Oh?"

"Yep. Your trouble is that you can't be argued out of your foolishness. And Bill," he said.

"Yes," I said, waiting.

"There's no hope for a man too foolish to know that he's a fool."

"Exactly," I said. "Good-night."

Six

The very next morning Tennie was over to apologize – for getting drunk.

"To tell you the truth," he said, "I don't remember a thing I said after the discussion about the separation of Quebec."

I told him that I did not remember talking about Quebec.

"We must have," he said. "We always do."

I looked at him closely. He was lying, of course. We had talked about the possible separation of the Province of Quebec as part of the Great Kitchen Debate on the Americanization of Canada.

"I should not allow myself to get that drunk," he continued. "I don't usually do that." And again he was lying. I have seen the piles of bottles which he empties *every week* into the trash-can.

But all of this was part of his plan: it's fairly clear. He pretends not to remember what he said at the party the night before. Therefore, it does not exist as far as he is concerned. He has erased it. But he leaves the image of what he said hanging in my mind. I was not drunk; I cannot pretend to have been drunk; therefore the image is now mine, and I am responsible for it. It was a very clever bit of manoeuvring.

"Bill," he said, "I want you to promise me one thing." He changed the tone of his voice so that I would know that the subject of his drunkenness and Corrie's secret was closed, put away, forgotten. He was on something new.

"What's that?" I said—understandably suspicious, I think.

"I want you to promise me that when you decide to sell this house, you'll tell me first."

I must have looked surprised. Did he think I was going to evict him after last night—mind you, he does not have a lease, of course.

He went on. "I don't expect you to give me an option or anything like that," he said. "I just want you to tell me when you decide to sell the place. I think I'd like to try to meet your price."

"Well," I said, "to tell you the truth, I had not thought of selling. I thought I would live here throughout the foreseeable future." Indeed, I have planned to die here, although I did not feel it necessary to go into that.

"Bill," he smiled at me. "You can't keep this place up."

"What do you mean?"

"The *upkeep*," he said, laughing as if I were too dim to understand the absolute clarity of his position.

"I am getting by," I said.

"But look," he said. "What about painting the place?"

"I told you that I'd buy the paint for you."

"I mean the *out*side."

"What about it?" I wanted to know.

"It's peeling," he said.

"It's not," I insisted. "Paint does not peel off shingles."

But he insisted that I tramp out into the snow with him, and so I did. He was quite right. The grey paint underneath the windows was peeling off the shingles under the duress of the hard winter.

"It'll be worse in the spring," he explained. "When the hot sun gets to it. It gets dried out, and peels. It's the drying out that does it." He acted as if he were being helpful.

"Well," I told him. "I guess I'll have to have it painted, then."

He wondered if I had any idea how much it would *cost* to have a house this size painted. I confessed that I had no idea.

Neither did he, he admitted. But he would predict a cost of at least $800 at a minimum. Perhaps it could cost over a thousand.

"I'll paint it myself," I suggested.

"Suit yourself," he said. "But it's a big job." He even argued that I would then be working for the house – rather than the house working for me.

He's a clever fellow – I'll give him that.

We went back into my kitchen, where I served him coffee. Then he sprang his next surprise on me. "Have you ever thought about getting a humidifier?"

No, I had not thought about getting a humidifier.

"Well, Jesus, Bill," he said, acting surprised, "isn't it getting to your furniture?"

I said that I did not know.

"Well, it's getting to mine," he said. "It's the weather up here." He then insisted that I accompany him to the living-room, where he would show me what he meant. And he very carefully picked out one of the weaker pieces of furniture — a rocking-chair which even the Secombes had considered too shaky to take with them, and which I had refinished with some care. He took hold of one of the supporting rungs between the rockers. Without much difficulty he pulled it loose. It wasn't broken of course; merely unglued.

"Everything is falling apart at my place, too," he said. "Did you notice my furniture last night?"

I remarked that I had not had the opportunity of sitting down last night.

Well, he informed me, all of the kitchen chairs squeaked. Every time you shifted your buttocks on those chairs, the damn things squeaked.

I thought that some glue might be a help, but he said that the glue wasn't the problem. It was the dryness of the air. What I needed, he said, was a humidifier.

And the gall of the man! He "just happened" to have some advertisements for humidifiers in his pocket. He had torn out the appropriate pages from both the Simpsons-Sears and the Eaton's catalogues.

The best kind for me, he had decided, was the humidifier which could be attached to the furnaces. He emphasized the plural. There *were* smaller ones, he admitted, but you had to look after the damn things all the time, and he doubted if — given the size and dried-out condition of the house — they would be very effective.

"When's Corrie coming back?" I asked.

"Next week," he said. And he began to tell me about the mice in the walls.

Now it is possible that there are mice in the walls, although it is my opinion that what we hear are merely squirrels running on the roof. I asked him if he had *seen* any mice.

He admitted that he had not.

Had he, perhaps, set any traps?

No, he had not done that, either.

Had he put out any poison?

No, he had not put out any poison. I was to remember, he said, that he had three children.

And, he continued, the lid of the toilet-tank was cracked — did I know that?

No, I did not know that. How did it happen?

He did not seem to know. It was just there — this morning, in fact. (So that was why he invited me to his party — to involve *me* in the party would absolve *him* from any damage resulting from it!) He had never noticed it before, but this morning when he had gone to flip the rubber-stopper-ball which somehow had failed to fall into its proper place (that too!) he had noticed the crack.

Well, I told him, I supposed that the replacement of toilet-tank tops was the landlord's responsibility. Did he see it that way?

He did not know — actually. Perhaps it was. Perhaps it *usually* was. He had never had to deal with anything like that before.

I began to be amused at him. Here he had marched over here this morning with the firm intention of shoving me into a place comfortable for *him*, but I had counter-attacked, and now he was merely shuffling.

"Well," I said, easily enough, "I'll get some glue and come over and glue it."

He said that there was no hurry, of course. It was not as if it had been the toilet-*bowl*. That would be expensive, he said. Not to mention the water damage.

I said that maybe he'd better not invite any fat friends to his house. He laughed and said that the only *fat* friend they had was Marie Pettipants, and he laughed when he mentioned her name.

Then he smiled knowingly at me and said: "Nope. Corrie and I and the kids are the only ones who use it."

He said that deliberately, just to let me imagine a glimpse of Corrie's rump, and invoke the picture of her which I had heard from his lips last night. And then the fellow smiled.

He had to get along home. "'Bye."

Corrie's back!

She and the boys arrived in a Sullivan's Taxi (Tennie did not even drive out to the airport to meet her), and when it stopped in front of the house I thought that perhaps nobody was home next door and perhaps I should go out to meet her. I even went so far as to put on my hat and coat and boots. But by that time she had paid the driver, and Jack and Robert were rushing up the half-shovelled walk and into the house. She had only the one small bag, and she began to pick her way through the snow toward their side of the house.

I started out the door, but Robert and Jack had obviously warned Tennie, who was at home after all. He appeared at their doorway and came out and stood on the front steps, grinning. Corrie ran to him. She dropped her bag and ran to him quite blatantly in broad daylight on Rodman Street.

"Oh, Tennie, I've *missed* you!" she shouted, loud enough for everyone in the neighbourhood to hear. Then she kissed him full on the lips, and snuggled into his shoulder.

He hugged her and swung her around, right off her feet, and carried her into the house. Just like in the movies.

When the telephone rang the next morning I thought it might be Corrie, but it was really too early for her to be up yet—she was undoubtedly tired from the trip. It was Tennie.

His voice was serious. Could I come over to his side of the house for a few minutes. He sounded austere, sure of himself.

I said: "Of course." I dressed and went over.

Tennie let me in. When I had taken off my boots and coat he said to me: "Bill, I've never complained before."

That was true, perhaps, in an obvious sense, and I

decided to agree with him. "That's true," I said.

"Well," he said, "I've got a complaint."

The house was quite quiet. I could hear no one stirring upstairs. "Well," I said, "what is it?"

"We've got cockroaches," he said.

I confess that I was astounded. Surely not, I thought. Not cockroaches. They are extremely difficult to get rid of once they settle in a house.

"How many?" I said.

"Only a few," he said. "That we could *see*," he added.

"And where were they?"

"In the kitchen."

"Perhaps I'd better take a look."

I began to think that perhaps it was all a joke, and half expected to walk into the kitchen and find it all laid for a surprise breakfast—with coffee and cream, danish rolls and blueberry muffins, and Corrie, smiling beside it all.

It was nothing like that at all. I followed Tennie into the kitchen, and found it a mess.

"Where are the children?" I asked.

"In school of course," he said.

"Robert?"

"Still asleep."

The breakfast table, a chrome-and-Formica affair, showed evidence of the children's breakfast. They had had toast and cereal for breakfast—the top of the table was still littered with crumbs and odd bits of Rice Krispies and Corn Flakes. The top of the toaster, which was sitting on the table, was greasy with little fingerprints. A nearly empty jar of York Peanut Butter was still on the table with its top off, the contents drying out. The jar of Robertson's Strawberry Jam was still open, too.

Then I heard Corrie behind me. She was standing in the doorway, still sleepy-eyed, wearing an old blue terry-cloth robe, and a cigarette dangled from her lips. She hadn't even washed her face yet, or combed her hair. Her eyes were still puffy.

"Hi, Bill," she smiled at me.

"Welcome back," I said.

"Thank you," she smiled.

"I understand you have some trouble," I said. Then, turning to Tennie, I inquired about the supposed residence of these fierce cockroaches.

"They were over there," he said, pointing a finger at the waste-basket. The waste-basket had a paper bag from the Dominion Store in it, and it was full to overflowing with coffee grounds, egg-shells, and, on the top, a half-eaten piece of toast.

"What did they look like?" I said.

"I don't know," said Tennie — and then, when I showed my exasperation, he said: "Small, black bugs. They scurried when I turned on the light."

"Black, you say."

"Reddish black," he said.

"Were there many?"

"I said there weren't many I could *see*," said Tennie.

"Where did they 'scurry' to?"

"Under the refrigerator."

I went over to the refrigerator and tapped on the sides with my fingers. Then I listened for the sound of small movements. There was nothing. Then I kicked lightly at the garbage basket, and listened again. Again there was nothing.

"Tennie," I said, "I think you're pulling my leg."

"No I am not," he said.

I looked at Corrie to see if she was about to break into a smile, but she had her back to me. She was at the stove, putting the coffee-pot on.

"Well," I said, "I suppose it's only natural."

"What?"

"Well, you know what they call cockroaches up here."

"No I do not," said Tennie.

"They do *not* call them cockroaches," I said.

"What's that got to do with it?"

"They call them Yankee Settlers."

"They don't."

"They do."

"I can't believe that," he said.

"Well, look it up," I said. "But if you want to be serious about it, I suggest that you keep your garbage covered."

And with that, I left them to their own devices.

Seven

Now!

I shall *not* give in.

THE ALIEN'S GUIDE TO SURVIVAL (Continued)

It is above all necessary to *avoid defeat*. This should be the Alien's first motto—as it was Adam's.

It should be admitted, of course, that the laws made by political bodies—whether they be parliaments, legislatures, or congressional assemblies—are enacted chiefly to maintain the popularity of the "representatives" of the "people". In short, politicians work to *stay in power*. Consequently, the laws are made for the benefit of the large, *inept majority*. Indeed, they are made in order to protect the member of the majority from the *consequences* of his own foolishness. For example, any man of *skill* and *foresight* will perceive the foolishness of marrying young because he realizes that such a decision will *restrict* the broad range of choices available to the *free* man. The man of *foresight* will discipline himself, and *wait*.

But your average man cannot wait. He will rush into marriage and into consequent employment – buy a house – shortly find himself unemployed and in debt. He will then demand that the government "look after" him, and he will go on the welfare rolls. He will sell his *soul* for the sake of his biological needs.

Thus, all legislation is written *in aid of* the *weak man*.

The extraordinary man, on the other hand, is subject chiefly to the laws of nature (birth and death) and is therefore comparatively *free*. If one locality (or nation) offends him, he moves to another and begins again.

And he is *able* to do *this* because of the *natural* superiority of his *wits*. Like Machiavelli, he knows that *survival* is a matter of *cunning* and *cleverness*.

As for *entertainment*, the superior man has the *free play* of his *mind*. He can "reason within the realm of possibility" – without which no scientific laws would ever have been *discovered*, nor any great books written. He is *free* to *choose* the *life of the mind*, and to play in the gardens of his *fancy*.

The superior man does this, and it separates him from his lesser companions as much as the *play* of certain members of the animal kingdom (bears and otters *play*, I believe) separates them from the lesser animals (moles).

Perhaps strangely, I first realized the potential of my mind when I accompanied my mother to Reverend Dobbs' services at Clifton's First Baptist Church. There were certain Sundays which I would have preferred to have missed (admittedly) — particularly those on which some of the younger members of the congregation were to be "accepted" into the church. That is, on certain Sundays the Reverend Dobbs would complete his friendly sermon and, when the final ceremonies had been completed, he would issue the call: "If there are any among you who wish to make Jesus Christ your Lord and Saviour, would you please come forward during the singing of the final hymn." Now, in the days of the Pentecostal Promise Church you can be sure that there would be at least a few who would come forth to be saved from the consequences of their week's activities. Indeed, there was one old lady who was saved quite regularly; heaven knows how much she must have stolen from the lady whose house she cleaned. But at the more "reputable" church, the words of Reverend Dobbs were no more than a vestige of the ancient ritual. When the young people came forward (in their *very best* clothes), you could be sure that it was all pre-arranged — and indeed, the water in the baptismal well was already warm.

But on such occasions — particularly on such occasions — when Reverend Dobbs wandered through his exemplary tales as a lineman for the telephone company — I sat beside my mother (in the haze of her perfume) and thought about food. For the fact is that Sunday dinner was always a grand affair with us. (You must know that among mid-western Baptists gluttony is not only *not* a sin; it is a positive *virtue.*) At the very least, I knew that when we got home my mother would serve us a meal of fried chicken, mashed potatoes (with heavy chicken gravy), peas, cooked carrots, chef's salad, and a dessert of coconut-cream pie.

So while Reverend Dobbs spoke on and on about the "common-sense" approach to Christianity, I thought about food. Indeed, I designed *restaurants.*

My favourite restaurant was of course one where everyone should be *comfortable.* I imagined it to be a large, deceptively grey building at the end of the main street. It would feature several *different* restaurants under *one* roof (and by buying in bulk, it would save on costs while offering a variety of menus to the patrons), and each restaurant would offer a special dish as a mark of its separate identity.

As one entered, one would be met by a gracious young woman—someone like Corrie!—who would make one "feel at home".

It would be the task of the hostess to inquire discreetly about your taste for the day. It would be her job to guide you to the *proper* room.

Because it was always a horror of my youth that I would be embarrassed. I had a constant fear of accompanying my mother into an attractive restaurant and then, horror of horrors, finding out that it was *too expensive*; or perhaps worse, finding out that it *served alcoholic beverages*, and my mother would feel obligated to leave before she was offended by some jolly, red-nosed fellow. One can imagine the *disgrace* of having to leave, walking out past all of those people who mocked our clothes—Cheap, Poor!—and beliefs. Or, having sat down at the table and received the menu, discovering only *then* that we could not afford the tariff. To go or stay? The bland young waitress hovering over us while my mother said, "We'll just have a salad—and coffee." Then making matters worse by saying: "We've already *eaten*." Oh, terrible! There is nothing worse in this world than humiliation.

And in reaction I would consider tearing the place to pieces, running amuck and kicking over tables, throwing silverware everywhere in astounding, flashing explosions.

Or I would imagine myself *alone*, and find it unnecessary to defend my mother. I am truly sorry for this.

When the gracious young woman with long brown hair met me at the door, she would know immediately that I was not wealthy, and know exactly the room for my appetites and pocket-book. She would suggest: "The Steak Room, sir?" And I would nod, and follow. She would guide me to the room where one could have a "set" dinner of charcoal-broiled steak, baked potato, garlic bread, tossed salad, and coffee, all for $1.19. My mother, perhaps, had been steered to the room which specialized in macaroni salad, for which she had a great fondness, along with potato salad—particularly "German" potato salad, with bits of bacon, made with vinegar and served hot.

Often, as the sermon ended, I allowed myself a few moments' thought on a more exotic restaurant. Oh, this too has come to pass! The room where only men like me were admitted. A room which specialized in sea food: french-fried shrimp in a basket, lobster, long platters each with a single fish. It was to be served by dark young waitresses who wore only sarongs, and only about their hips. Ah, as the picture of this room was created before my eyes I felt the stirrings of my appetites.

And I was then ready to hear the Reverend Dobbs say, "Let us rise for the last hymn, and remain standing for the benediction." "Holy, Holy, Holy" rang out as we welled up in song along with the Hammond Electric Organ.

Then he would issue the call, and the young people would shuffle forward with uncertain feet and the pretence of joyful decision in their eyes. We would sit through the dunking (the floor was lifted, and there was the pool; Reverend Dobbs wore a special robe—although hip-waders would have been more appropriate), and my stomach rumbled.

As we left the church, Mother would say, sadly, "Aren't you going to join them some day soon?" and I would mumble something. Of course I finally *did*, in order to be with Katherine, but I did not give in easily. That faith too easily assumed is too easily lost.

"I have a surprise for you," Mother said.

"What's that?"

"Something you'll like."

"What's that?"

"Rolled veal roast — with gravy." My heart leapt and my mouth watered. Then she continued, "And acorn squash."

I hated acorn squash. "But you must *learn* to like it," smiled Mother.

When I met Corrie in the basement today, she was *diffident*. Yes, that is the word. She seemed determined to "keep her distance", almost as if she had been ordered to do so. Nor is it surprising. Tennie, having realized that what I overheard might be dangerous, has given Corrie certain *rules* and *instructions*. For example, when I asked her about her trip — for we've had no opportunity to discuss it — she replied in only the most general (and genial) terms. No, there had been no difficulties with her brothers. No, nothing "untoward" had happened during the arrangements for the funeral. And when I asked her if she had found things much changed at home, hoping that she would tell me something about her childhood (for I feel that I do not yet know her as well as I ought), she replied only that she hadn't lived "at home" in so long that it had not meant much for her to return. Were there no neighbours who remembered her? She shook her head — as if to say that she had remembered them, but they had not remembered her. I know that feeling. But surely, I suggested, a large family like that — it must be a *close* family. No, apparently that was not true. Apparently large families are no closer than small ones, perhaps even less. She said that she had always been given leave to go pretty much her own way. Corrie stayed over by the washing machine and dryer, so that I had to stand at the grill like a prisoner, trying to talk to her.

For one moment I thought she might come closer. I had begun to talk about my youth in Clifton in order to show her why I had drunk so little liquor at Tennie's party, and she started toward me — then changed her mind, picked up her broom (which had slid and fallen from its place by the washing machine), and began to sweep the area around her laundry machines. I wondered *to myself* if Tennie had told her about that party. If he had, he might well have given her some orders—"Corrie, you stay away from our landlord"—*in order to protect himself.*

"Corrie," I said, "did Tennie tell you about his party?"

She grinned at me. "He said he had a few friends in. How did you like Miss Pettipants?"

"Her!" I said.

"Isn't she *awful*?" laughed Corrie.

But then she went back upstairs. I watched her go and thought that perhaps I ought to buy her some clothes if Tennie wouldn't. It would be an outrageous step, of course, but one comes to the outrageous decision sometimes, *of necessity*. Tennie seems to have bought his wife nothing but blue jeans, sweatshirts, and the occasional dress for travelling.

It is true that I have always been prey to mysterious illnesses—viruses, mostly—and the spring seems to have released these illnesses into the air to get their hold on me. I feel heavy with illness, for example, weighed down, as if I had gone through some difficult emotional experience. But if my body seems weighty and ponderous, my head feels light—even playful.

Thus, more for my own amusement than anything else, I lie on my bed and pretend to be dying.

Outside I notice that the snowbanks, smooth and neatly sheared along the road by the snow-blowers, have rotted into immense ugly shapes: monuments of filth. Piles of sand are revealed, cinders, cigarette packages, bottles, candy-wrappers, dog-droppings: all decomposing in this ill springtime. I have not been outside, of course, in days.

No, I am lying here pretending to be dying. The house is overheated, as it so often is, and I twist and turn in the hot, damp sheets in the surprising sunshine which streams in through my bedroom window. Tennie has turned up the heat too high again.

I twist in the ropes of my stinking sheets (I am strung out on ropes; it is an ancient torture), and groan. I groan very loudly sometimes, although, in the interests of reticence and decorum, I try not to let my groans develop into bellows of pain.

Corrie is over there alone. Or at least, she is over there in silence while Robert is having his nap. I heard her put him down (screaming, of course) two hours ago.

I groan from the pit of my stomach, and find it enjoyable. I push the air up from my abdomen, constrict it in the rib cage, and push it out like a mental defective who is attempting, desperately, to talk. I babble in groans.

Perhaps I groan so that Corrie will hear me and come, finally, to my door, hammering on it with tears in her eyes to ask, "Bill, what *is* it, for God's sake?"

Perhaps her hair will be loose, blown by the harsh spring breeze. Her face will be cold and shiny from the season. Her brown eyes warm and liquid from bewilderment. The wind will keep her fresh.

When she knocks at the door, I shall pull myself from my bed. I am naked, of course, and my slack body is a sack of falling muscles.

I groan, groan, groan. It feels good to toss my head back and forth, to ensure that the rhythm is irregular.

Groan, groan, groan.

And, naked in front of the mirror in the hallway, I suck in my gut and put on a hat. I bought the hat years ago—it has a large bunch of feathers, like a shaving-brush—because it made me look like that good fellow, Bing Crosby. He's very old now. I even tried a pipe for a week or two, but it seemed to have little or no effect.

With my hat on, I look relatively young.

No. There are deep furrows in my face. I look like an ape with a hat on.

There is a funny story of which I am very fond. Once there was a man who walked around his house naked all day, except that he wore a hat. On one occasion a friend of his dropped by. The friend, needless to say, was somewhat astounded. "My dear fellow," said the friend, "you are stark naked." "Yes," replied the fellow. "That's true. But it doesn't matter. Nobody ever comes to visit me."

"But, then — why are you wearing the hat?"

"Well," said the fellow. "You never know when someone might drop by."

I shall tell you something: it feels *good* to groan.

I have just caught myself *giggling*. Now then, Mr. William Boyd, none of that! That will never do. Nor will you allow yourself a single *howl*. A howl would be too much.

I have also pretended that I am a prisoner in this room, at least until this virus passes from me. I have tried to count all the little pebbles in the wall of the room; the walls are genuine plaster-and-lath, as James Secombe so proudly asserted. Of course it is a difficult business: one can never remember where one started. This surprises me because it throws a new light on the life of a prisoner. Even a prisoner can be confused.

That is very interesting.

When I have found it necessary to interrupt my groaning to answer a call of nature and visit the toilet, I try to walk with a heavy, stumbling step. You can feel the irregular, sick vibrations throughout the house. If I keep this up, of course, I shall leave hand-marks all over the walls. They will be somewhat lower than they would be if I were walking erect. Obviously, I descend in my movements. Like an ape. Ha!

Lately it seems to me that I have heard Corrie and Tennie arguing more than before. Perhaps it is that my "illness" has simply given me the time to give my attention to it. The arguments storm upstairs and downstairs — becoming more restrained only when they near the area of my groaning.

It gave me a certain pleasure, yesterday, to cut Tennie short. He was storming up the stairs after Corrie, bellowing in exasperation, "Jesus Christ, Corrie, Jesus Christ!"

I groaned.

He shut up.

It was the last week of my teaching career. I did not know that at the time, of course, although I suspected it. I planned to resign, but I thought that I should wait until the *last moment*. It would leave Schneider in an awkward position, and he deserved that, at the very least. But if I am truthful with myself, and I always am, I would have to admit that I believed that they were trying to find some way of easing me out. It would be difficult, of course. I never made any fuss, I fulfilled all the requirements (and, I daresay, I was more competent than the nincompoops who insisted that we were all "colleagues" together), and of course I avoided anything which might have given them the chance to dismiss me on the grounds of moral turpitude. Certainly I have always been chaste. Yet there was always that fact on my dossier, in the area reserved for Marital Status. Check one, it says: Single, Married, Separated, Divorced. I had to check the Divorced category, of course, although to my mind I had never been married. I have always thought of myself as single. I do not remember Katherine and I ever sharing a breakfast (she slept late the entire month, hiding from me in the bed), or even going shopping together on a Friday night. None of the domestic activities. And the irony of it was that if I had remarried I would have been safely ensconced in that "Married" category; the "Divorce" would have been erased. So Schneider must have looked at my application with some doubts in his mind. Divorced—and not remarried—and thirty-nine years old. Also against me was the fact that my grades in college were *too high*, except in Education courses. Superintendents and Principals are wary of the likes of me. They actually prefer to hire stupid teachers — who will not be, as they say, "over the heads of the lads and lassies". But of course they were hiring me late in the year, and they were desperate. I had left my last post at the last moment, just as I did this one. And all they could say against me were the usual things: "Mr. Boyd is perhaps uncooperative; he does not take an active part in the life of the community; his teaching seems quite adequate."

That sort of thing: nothing against, but nothing for.

But I *always* covered myself. Even during the last week of school, when I knew that Schneider was rattling his little brain back and forth, trying to find a way to get rid of me. Even though I had already packed all my belongings into a trunk, ready to move on to my final destination — which, of course, turned out to be here: Fredericton, New Brunswick, the City of Stately Elms, which has a fine old Loyalist Graveyard. Those previous unbelievers in the sanctity of the Great Democratic Unwashed Will are buried there. I, too, shall be buried in Fredericton, also a man of choice, decision, wisdom.

But Schneider would have been glad to get me fired, and I sometimes wonder if the incident with the boy wasn't part of his plan. I do not believe he had the brains to be capable of duplicity, however. He was condemned to a certain dog-like honesty. But he would have *taken advantage* of the opportunity if the incident had developed into anything. Still, the school *was* strangely deserted.

I had finished cleaning out my desk and, indeed, I believe that I was the only one left in the building, although I thought that I heard the sound of the janitor knocking his broad broom into the far corners of the second-floor corridor, far away. He could have served as a witness, presumably. And I came down the stairs with my little satchel full of paper-clips, note-cards, and class records. (One *always* holds onto one's records; that way the School Board must pay up.)

The boy was loafing against the doors of the school. He was not very tall; and he was dressed with that careful anonymity which high-school students insist upon, whatever the fashion of the time and place. He wore jacket, jeans, and shoes: our local uniform. His face was that of the usual adolescent: grotesque and unformed, unsettled, dangerous.

I asked him, please, to move aside. I wished to go out the door. The ridiculousness of the situation was not lost on me: here we were, two people in a virtually empty building, and in one another's way. He moved very slowly, and I asked him what he was doing there.

"I'm waiting for somebody."

"Who?"

"Somebody."

"Well," I said. "You're not supposed to be in the building after four o'clock. You must wait outside."

"It's cold outside."

"It's not that cold."

"I'd rather wait here."

"You're not supposed to be here. Wait outside."

"No."

"What?"

"No."

"Look," I said patiently, "get outside."

"No."

Perhaps I started toward him, or made some gesture which he thought was sufficiently threatening for his interpretation.

"Go on," he said, "hit me."

"What?"

"Hit me," he said. "Hit me and I'll have you fired."

It was true. We were not allowed to lay a hand on the

little beasts. It was like training lions by rational persuasion.

"You'll get your ass fired," he said.

"What did you say?"

"I said you'll get fired."

"That's not what you said."

"Sure it is."

He stuck to his story.

I have been working lately on my series of letters to the editors of various newspapers. They are of course part of my campaign to *induce* attitudes by causing reflection. I was writing one which I planned to send to the Fredericton *Daily Gleaner*, the Toronto *Star*, and the Montreal *Star*, arguing that the current "student rebellion" was utter nonsense. I was concentrating on the popular analogy of the "student" to "nigger". What nonsense! A student can always *quit*. The "student", I pointed out, always has a choice: "To be or not to be" a student. It is not a condition of his birth. He can always go find a job digging ditches and "do his thing" to his heart's content.

Now, for reasons of my own, I prefer to do my work by candlelight. Indeed, I bought a couple of tall brass candlesticks from Budovich's Second-Hand store, and found them quite satisfactory. Of course I am quite careful with them. Is their use an indication of an eighteenth-century mind? Perhaps so. At any rate, Fredericton is an eighteenth-century place, blessedly untouched by the industrial revolution. But, as I say, I was working on my letters when I heard a pounding on my front door.

I went downstairs quickly and opened the door just a crack (keeping it on its chain) because, although I was wearing my hat, I was "as Nature made me".

It was Corrie and Tennie.

Corrie was saying, "Bill—are you all right?"

"Of course," I said.

"We thought we saw fire." They were passing by, and, looking up, saw the flickering of my candles.

"Fire?"

"From your windows."

"I'm working by candlelight," I said.

"Oh," they said together.

"Yes," I said.

"We thought we'd better ask," said Corrie, smiling.

I thanked them for their interest, and they left. Of course I quite understood. Her curiosity is beginning to work, just as I have intended. Is that not what *education* is all about? To incite curiosity? Now she was beginning to be interested.

And Tennie, I perceived from his expression, was beginning to wish that perhaps he had struck me physically that night at the party. I was entirely too dangerous for him. He thought that he would simply *intimidate* me with his insults, but he picked on the wrong man. It would have been better for him to have followed his natural (violent) inclinations.

Then I went back to my work, and began to draft a second letter—for the Saint John *Telegraph-Journal,* the Toronto *Globe* & *Mail,* and the Halifax *Chronicle-Herald,* pointing out that we have come to the point in our civilization where we must *decide* on *what quality* of life we desire. Do we wish to have the paper-mills pollute our rivers and streams (as the Americans have done, everywhere), in order that we may have bigger and better K-Marts? Or do we wish to "change our way of living" and have a life which is less oriented toward the manufacturing and consuming of goods? The choice is clearly before us, and perhaps we had better *make* that choice before the industrialists *take over* our society entirely (and thus make life not worth living), or some revolutionaries take to *blowing up* the industrial plants.

Lately Corrie is angry just as often as Tennie. I hear her.

Perhaps she has come to realize (since the death of her mother) that she is growing old like everyone else, and will not always have that firm, slightly plump figure which looks so good in blue jeans. Perhaps she examines herself in the morning before her mirror and discovers that, despite the fact that she bottle-fed her three children, they have none the less taken their toll on her.

And one particular morning lately she was in a fine rage, and it was such a diffuse argument that, even with my ear to the wall, it was difficult to follow. The gist of it was that the children were on her nerves. Of course.

It was a Saturday, I believe, and the night before, she and Tennie had had a long and involved discussion about the "housing situation". She wanted to buy a house, apparently, and he argued that the time was not ripe, that prices and interest rates were too high—"too damned high"—and at the very least they ought to be goddamned sure that they were going to stay in Canada. What if all the winters were like this one? (Indeed, according to all the statistics in the encyclopedia, this has been a perfectly average winter.) But although Tennie's position seemed to me to be quite a reasonable one, Corrie was in no mood to accept it reasonably. Darling Corrie is often restive.

And on that particular morning—yes, it was certainly Saturday—the children were all in the living-room watching the television cartoons. It is one of the best times of the week for children. They do not caterwaul; only the television set does.

But somehow or other Corrie was offended by their very lack of activity. There they were, sitting in their mess of cookies, comics, and assorted half-eaten fruit, their eyes on the cartoon adventures of "Archie and His Friends".

No amount of urging from Corrie would send them out to play in the cold sunshine. In vain did she plead with them. She pointed out that the exercise would be good for them. Did they want to turn into slugs? In vain she argued that they ought to play outside when they could. They were in school *all week;* maybe next weekend it would be *raining* — or "snowing again".

In vain she condemned the vapidity of the television cartoon.

Once she even turned off the set in a fit of pique. Alisha and Jack protested, and were smacked for their trouble. Robert was more difficult to deal with. The smacking merely invoked a greater howl from him: he was not only being deprived of his TV; he was also being hurt. He howled until Corrie was in tears of rage and she turned the set back on. Totally defeated by her children and the culture.

Then of course Tennie came thundering down from his study to ask just what in hell was the racket all about.

"Well, why *can't* they watch TV?"

Corrie was unable to explain.

When she did, finally, in a kitchen conference, it did her no credit. She confessed to Tennie — and to herself — that she herself remembered "Archie and His Friends". She had read the comic books, and what's more, when she was a child she had listened to "Archie and His Friends" on the radio on Saturday mornings.

Tennie had *no sympathy* with her. He told her that she ought to be ashamed of herself, and she wept and said she was. She was so ashamed.

Her period must have been due.

It is necessary for me to be careful when I follow their arguments through the house. What if one day they stopped, and Tennie said to Corrie: "Look, speak more quietly, will you? That sonofabitch Boyd is probably listening."

Therefore I often crawl through the house on my hands and knees, listening at the baseboards.

Although it gives me great pleasure, of course, to see my letters printed (and I often go down to Mazzuca's to buy the out-of-town papers; I am considering expanding my operations to the West Coast, endeavouring to save Canada from the fate of the United States), I confess that I also find a great deal of pleasure in imagining the reaction in an editorial office when one of them arrives. I can imagine the look on the face of the editor when he receives my letter. The letter, of course, assaults all the *popular* beliefs from which the newspaper makes its money. I can see the editor calling all his minions around him to read my letter—"Would you believe what Boyd is saying *this* time?"—and all of the sub-editors, the reporters, and the typists, turning away with appropriate chuckles and giggles.

But what I have said nags in their minds. They are unable to refute me; unable to forget me. I suspect that I have a rather large following.

Of course I receive a good deal of "crank" mail, because I always include my name and address, and allow the newspapers to print both.

If the writers of the crank letters include their addresses, I simply write a postcard in return. I say: THINK AGAIN. If I receive a subsequent unreasonable attack on me, I write a card which says: THINK AGAIN, IF YOU CAN.

Some of these people have been persuaded to my point of view.

Others, of course, do not reveal their addresses, and these people simply send me obscene notes and inform me (variously) that I ought to be shot, tortured, hanged, or educated. Luckily, they do not know I am an American, or they would suggest that I ought to be deported. One J. R. Roberts of Willawawn Drive, Halifax, has made that suggestion anyway.

But it is enough for the present if I can put a burr under the saddled consciousness of the great muddled masses.

Later, when I have finished my book, we can begin to move toward more formal organizations.

By Nature:
Richard Milhous Nixon is a Used-Car Salesman.
Lyndon Baines Johnson was a Snake-Oil Salesman.
Dwight David Eisenhower was an Insurance Salesman.
John Diefenbaker was a Feed Salesman.
Lester Pearson was a Solicitor of Contributions for the United Appeal.

Pierre Elliott Trudeau is a special case. I see him as a disinherited European aristocrat with a papal title who has married money and done well by it. I rather admire him; he is restoring the Monarchy. Of course, it is *his own*.

Sometimes I truly despair of civilization. I was preparing to go to the bank (and was therefore dressed; Corrie and Tennie had slipped out to the grocery) when there was a sudden and persistent ringing of my doorbell. I answered it, and there was a little fellow—about Jack's age, I should guess—staring up at me with round, hopeful eyes. He thrust a sheaf of papers at me and asked me if I would like to buy some magazines. It appeared that he was selling magazine subscriptions as part of a campaign to raise money for the school library. If his class sold a number of subscriptions to magazines (which I, for one, did not want) then the school library would receive a certain amount of money from the magazine distributor.

The hopefulness of the child tore at my heart; the nastiness of the scheme outraged me. It was a new wrinkle, but an old trick. Send the kiddies out to work for some commercial venture, but dress it up in some pseudo-philanthropical veil so that their soft and pitiful selling becomes virtuous *in itself*, and we, the public, buy what we do not want or need for the sake of the child. Back in Toronto somewhere there was the agent of an American firm raking in the shekels.

Sadly I told the sad little child that I did not want any of his magazines, and he went on down the street, humming hopefully. I wanted to weep for him and tear out somebody's throat.

I wrote a letter to the School Board.

> Gentlemen:
>
> I am willing to have my taxes raised, and I am willing to donate money to a library fund, but I resent your sending out the children to sell magazines for the profits of a commercial organization. Have you calculated the cost in man-hours to the school system for this? Have you calculated the cost of the administrative work done by the over-worked teachers as they pore over the endless forms and tot up the monies collected by the children? The teacher's time is worth *something*, you know. A teacher is a teacher—not an accounting clerk. I know—and I have collected money for various specious projects in all of the miserable school systems in which I taught for several years. To use child labour for commercial profit! Think of the child who comes to school in tears because he has not been able to reach his quota, because he has been unable to coerce his neighbours into buying something they don't want or donating to something they do not believe in. What if his parents, the chief targets of these campaigns, cannot afford to subscribe or donate? You should be ashamed.
>
> I am also writing to my M.L.A. Rest assured that this matter will be investigated and pursued.
>
> Sincerely yours,
>
> William A. Boyd
> 696 Rodman Street
> Fredericton, N.B.

But then, that very afternoon, something else happened.

Corrie and Tennie had gone out to escape my death, having decided, apparently, that I should be allowed to die in peace and loneliness, and they would ask the Fredericton Police Department to look in on my house in a couple of days, saying, "We mailed him his cheque – he preferred to be paid by cheque sent through the mail – only last week." But then, as I say, that very afternoon I made my way downtown to Colonel Sanders Kentucky Fried Chicken (there was a "special"), and there was quite a line-up. I chose my queue, and waited my turn. A woman came in – a plump, motherly, none-too-well-dressed woman – and took a place in the line behind me. Then, thinking that the next line over was moving more rapidly, she moved over there.

As it happened, we reached the counter at virtually the same moment. But when the young waitress in her candy-striped costume raised her eyebrows for the woman's order, the woman said: "I believe this gentleman here was here before me."

I was touched. I said, "Thank you."

But I was relieved to get my box of chicken and french fries and flee home before anything else upsetting took place. Luckily I was back before Corrie and Tennie, and was well-fed, naked, and groaning by the time I heard their VW putter up.

I lie in my sweating bed late – and I groan. Tennie leaves for the university, cursing and kicking at the slushy, rotting snow. Alisha and Jack have escaped – apparently before I woke up. I can hear Tennie saying, "For God's sake, Corrie, get them out of the house before he wakes up!" Perhaps the children have asked awkward questions, for which he has no answers.

After a brief, initial period of moaning, I restrict myself to silence for most of the morning. When Corrie turns on her vacuum cleaner I nip downstairs for coffee and cream, and return to my bed, naked, to drink it.

Then she has her turn at silence.

It is afternoon. Alisha and Jack have been home for lunch, and have returned to school. Robert has been put to bed for his nap, and Corrie and I remain in silence. I allow the silence to settle in over the house, allow the afternoon to be perfectly still (you can hear only the dust falling gently through the rays of sunshine) in order to breed thoughts in Corrie's lovely head. I think them—and it is just possible ("There are more things possible, Horatio," etc.) that they drift over to torment her as well.

Of course I hear her coming. I hear her pace the floor in indecision, full of thoughts and images, hear her make the decision and take her coat from the hall closet, hear her open the front door—pause in fear—then close it. I know exactly the time it will take her to reach my door, and I am already out of bed and putting on my old dressing-gown when I hear Corrie knock at the door.

The question is: to wear the hat or not to wear the hat? If I wear the hat, I look younger, and I can tell her the joke. It might well intrigue her. On the other hand, once the joke is told, the hat must be discarded, and there would be a loss of effect. I decide against the hat.

Without it I look gaunt and ill—but faintly evil and romantic.

Fantasy is the only freedom available to a dying man.

She is at my door, and I open it to see her standing sadly there—as if *summoned.*

Did she come of her own free will?

Yes, she did.

She says: "How are you, Bill?"

"Just fine, just fine." Indicating my old robe, I say, "Excuse my lack of dress."

She waves the problem aside. She's tired of thinking about it.

"We thought you might be ill."

"A little," I say. "Perhaps—well, yes, I guess I've been ill."

She looks at me closely—as if I might be playing a joke on her.

"You haven't shaved," she says, "but you don't *look* all that ill."

"Ah, I am, I am," I reply. "I'm dying," I announce sadly. She agrees. We are all dying, wearily.

"Could I have a cup of coffee?" she asks in her plaintive voice. "I'm very nervous today."

"Of course," I say. I hasten to the task—which doesn't take long because the instruments and ingredients for making coffee are always ready to hand.

I serve the coffee. She drinks it nervously, sitting on the edge of the chair as if determined to leave at the first opportunity. It is strange that she does not notice that I'm neither groaning nor coughing.

Her first comments are expected, but banal. One of them is to the effect that when she married Tennie she signed her death warrant for life. I remark that it is a "pretty phrase". She replies that she has "rehearsed it often enough".

But, she laments, she can think of no particular *thing* in which Tennie has failed her. And isn't it strange, she says, that divorce laws always seem to demand some *fact* of failure. Even the new ones ask "Why did the marriage fail?" and she realizes that they often fail for no particular reason. Tennie is good to her. He supports her well. He doesn't drink or gamble or seduce the girls in his classes, she believes. It is merely—she pauses to look at me with wan understanding over her cup of coffee—it is merely that he is somehow *inadequate*.

And the children! The children are perfectly normal—I must recognize that (I nod)—but the fact is that they are simply always *there*. She gestures her hopelessness. One can't say, can one, that one will fly to London tomorrow—even if one has the money. She complained that she was tied to Jack's Cub Pack and Alisha's figure-skating lessons.

I told her that I had noticed that she seemed to be nervous.

Yes, she was. Weren't we a fine pair—her with her bad nerves, me slipping away to death? We were a fine pair.

She spills her coffee! Her hands suddenly tremble so badly that the cup jiggles in the saucer, she reaches to steady it with her left hand, her cigarette starts to slip from her red mouth, and the brown coffee pours over her hand and onto the coffee table, drips on the rug! "Oh!" she cries out. She wails. She sits there in tears while I rush for a dish-cloth.

I mop it up.

I take one of her cigarettes, light it for her, and put it in her mouth. "Be calm," I say. She is weeping.

Then, with an attitude of taking command (such things are necessary), I say that she must obey me. If I have no cure, then at least I can offer therapy.

Her brown eyes are full of tears, as if pleading.

"The nerves' ills deserve the nerves' pleasures," I say.

What do I mean by that? she asks. She knows perfectly well what I am talking about. But I am cagey. I say: "Perhaps you ought to take a bath."

"Here?"

"Why not?"

She smiles. It is a crazy idea—but why not? Miraculously, she has agreed.

She stands up—and remembers. "What about Robert?"

"I'll listen for him," I say. "I can hear him."

She proceeds to the stairs, and refrains from giving me her little smile—until she has begun to climb the stairs.

I hear the water running, and I put the cups and saucers in the sink. She turns the water off; the pipes do not rattle. There is silence in the house.

Then I hear her get out of the tub. She is drying herself. I hear her open the door of the bathroom. I am standing at the foot of the stairs. I hear her bare feet moving softly on the carpet of the hallway. The smell of her bath, the natural perfume of her body, are in the air. She is standing at the top of the stairs, wrapped in a towel, looking at me.

She says gently: "Bill?"

I lie in my bed and groan, and shake with the fever of mortality. I am dying.

Tennie is in a terrible rage. When I was a boy, I naturally read all the usual "boys' stories". They were very jolly stories about boys in schools where boys wore uniforms. Of course, I have never seen such a school. And the boys were always playing pranks and escaping and hiding candy and the like. Bullies always got their come-uppance in the end.

But in one which I have long forgotten, there was a phrase which I have not forgotten. One boy said to another (about the teacher — or was it the Headmaster): "He's in a terrible wax." I immediately thought of a man wrapped in wax, and he looked rather like a black figure wrapped in the kind of wax which was used to make "moustaches" and "false teeth", and which, after wearing for a while, one chewed. But now, of course, I wonder where that phrase came from. Was it originally "He waxed wroth"? Does it have something to do with the "waxing and waning of the moon"?

But: Tennie was in a terrible wax.

And of course, when Tennie is in a rage he is very American — violent, vindictive, and unreasonable.

The facts which *caused* the rage are simple ones. Some weeks ago Jack had begged to be allowed to join a Cub Pack. Corrie was amenable, but Tennie was not too sure about the ethical goodness of the organization. *He* had been a Cub Scout once – but only for a couple of weeks. And anyway, the entire Scout organization was a "paramilitary" organization. "Paramilitary" was a word which appeared often in his conversation when he talked about society.

But now Jack had decided that he did not wish to attend the Cub meetings any more. They "gave orders and stuff". Tennie was outraged. Jack had begged for a Cub cap, shirt, and belt. He had paid his registration fee. Tennie had told him at the time that he had to make up his mind once and for all, and Jack said he had decided. He wanted to join. Now he had changed his mind; he didn't want to go.

Well, he was damn well *going* to go!

Jack was crying. Corrie pointed out softly that it was too late for him to go *now*, anyway. The meeting started at 6.30.

Jack sobbed that perhaps his father could drive him.

Tennie waxed wroth at the suggestion. He did not intend to become a goddamned chauffeur for his son. He told Jack to get on his Cub outfit and get the hell out of the house. Jack whimpered and whined, and Tennie hit him. Jack left, slamming the door. My side of the house shook as well.

Corrie asked Tennie if he didn't want her to leave as well.

Just what the hell did she mean by that?

Well, he didn't seem to like any of them any more. Perhaps she had better leave.

Tennie said that he had not *said* that.

Corrie replied that he seemed to *mean* that.

Tennie said he was responsible only for what he said.

Corrie said he must hate her.

Tennie was in a great wax. He damned, cursed, swore at her. He had the vocabulary of a sailor. He told her to damn well stop *cringing*. He couldn't stand people who cringed. Like that groaning sonofabitch next door, scared shitless by life.

Corrie murmured something I didn't hear, and then I heard Tennie breaking up the furniture. The kitchen chairs – "loosened" no doubt by the lack of humidity in the house, for which I was supposed to be responsible – were the first to go. They were smashed on the floor. You can imagine the shattering of them as Tennie brought them down from over his head with his immense strength. I once saw James Magee kill a harmless cow snake like that. He flailed it against the barn floor until its skull split, and it was nothing more than a dripping tube of gore.

Then, apparently, Tennie threw the supper on the floor – because Corrie screamed a single vile word – and then there was silence. That ominous silence.

I heard her leave the house.

I groaned.

Tennie said: "Boyd, you sonofabitch. . . . "

Some night I'll do for that man. Some night I shall put on my dark woollen cap, my navy-blue turtleneck sweater, and my dark blue wool trousers. I'll put socks *over* my shoes to muffle my footsteps. I shall blacken my face with burnt cork. There must be a cork around here somewhere. I shall purchase a cheap baseball bat at Canadian Tire. No, I shall order a cheap baseball bat from Simpsons-Sears, and cut it off and paint it black. No, I shall go over to Queen's Square and watch a game and pick up one of the broken bats which is left carelessly behind, trim it, and paint it black. I'll catch Tennie some evening and, like a commando, I'll bash him up good in the dark.

By mail-order I have purchased some very good bond notepaper. It has my name and address printed on the top—printed *as if* by an engraving process. Coughing and hacking, I write a brief note to Professor Harrison T. Cord.

Dear Professor Cord:

I am afraid that due to rising prices and costs of production it has become necessary for me to increase the cost of my product. Therefore, beginning with next month, the rent of your portion of my house will be raised by $99. The next rent due will be $299. (Two hundred and ninety-nine dollars, Canadian.)

May I remind you that you have no lease, and that I am unimpressed by violence. Your family does not seem to have this advantage.

Sincerely yours,

William A. Boyd
696 Rodman Street
Fredericton, N.B.

I did not date the letter; I merely await a reply.

The evening is mellow and warm. Spring is beginning to break out. Even with the sun down, the evening is surprisingly warm and fragrant. Somewhere I smell the sweet bloom of lilacs. I do not know of any lilac bush near by. I have drunk too much coffee today. My nerves are alive.

I lie naked in my bed and groan in the sweaty sheets.

The house is quiet. Tennie and the children have gone off somewhere. Corrie is alone in the other side of the house.

My thoughts, like a magician's, hover in the air. I let them breed in Corrie's yearning mind.

I hear her coming. I hear her pace the floor in indecision, afraid to come—and yet, unwilling not to. I hear her open the front door, pause, and then close it. I know exactly the time it will take her to reach my door, and I am already out of bed and putting on my old robe when I hear her timid knock.

Did she come of her own free will?

Yes, she did.

She says: "How are you, Bill?"

"Just fine, just fine," I say. Indicating my old robe, I say, "Excuse my lack of dress."

She waves the problem aside.

"We thought you might be ill," she says.

"I'm dying, I'm afraid."

"We all are," she says gently.

"Could I have a cup of coffee?" she says suddenly. "I'm very nervous today."

"Of course," I say, and I serve her the coffee.

She sits on the edge of the chair, as if ready to leave at the first mistake. She does not notice that, for the first time in weeks, I have ceased to cough and moan.

She begins by saying, wryly, that when she married Tennie she signed her death warrant for life. I return her sad smile.

But isn't it sad, she says, that marriages have to fail for some *reason*. Hers has failed, and yet she cannot blame Tennie, really. Of course he has a completely ungovernable temper—but she has an ungovernable capacity for weeping. He rages; she weeps. "It's just the way we are."

But the trouble is—that *that* is not *only* the way they are. She feels as if life has come to an end, that there is no future any more. The children bottle her up in the house and in their affairs until she feels that she will explode. And Tennie—Tennie is no *relief*. She wants to scream out for something *other*.

Her hands are shaking, and suddenly she spills her coffee. She has just put a cigarette in her mouth, and her right hand is shaking so much that she cannot control her cup, and when she tries to bring the saucer to it, her left hand shakes—and then her cigarette falls from her mouth, and she spills her coffee down the front of her soft grey dress.

She cries out—and then falls into uncontrollable weeping as I fetch paper towels from the kitchen and begin to mop up.

I tell her that perhaps she ought to take off her dress. And why not take a hot bath—it will calm her nerves.

"Here?" she asks quietly.

"Why not?"

With a soft smile of acquiescence, she agrees. As she turns to go upstairs to the bathroom I tell her that the flesh's pleasures are the only answer to the flesh's ills. That's not a cure, I say: it's only therapy. She turns to smile at me, and then goes.

Trembling, I listen to the water running through the pipes. Then she turns off the water and I know that she is resting—and weeping—in the bath. Then I hear the water being released. She is drying herself. Then the door opens, and I hear her soft footsteps on the hall carpet.

"Bill?" she calls.

She is nude at the top of the stairs.

I climb to her.

My eyes follow her like a camera as she leads me to the bedroom. Her dimpled rump.

I . . .

She assumes her favourite posture on the bed—Tennie was right, of course—and smiles back at me over her shoulder.

She says quietly: "Come on. I'm just like whipped cream. One push and you go right in."

To the Editor, Saint John *Telegraph-Journal*, etc., etc.:

> Dear Sir:
>
> We have been wrong for years. We have always assumed that love is the answer to our problems, that if Christian love (to use one example) could only be

adopted, then we should all be able to live with one another and indeed, if we believed *hard enough*, death itself would be eliminated, and we would once more find ourselves in the Garden of Eden. Through the love of Christ, man would no longer be a fallen creature. Or, we have believed that if Freudian love (the mutual attraction of the mating lust) were fulfilled, we should at least be content in our roles as fallen, human creatures.

As a result we have come to delude ourselves that love is the answer to death. As animals copulate to achieve the reproductive continuation of the species, so have we. We love for the sake of immortality, one way or another. We copulate for the future; we copulate for glory.

Copulation, fornication, adultery, then — are merely means of trying to live forever.

However, we now see that we are choking ourselves with love, that too much love has so choked the earth with people (the expanding population has resulted in a fatal human-induced pollution) that unless we cease to reproduce ourselves, we shall destroy the very species we have been trying to preserve forever. Man is the only animal whose intelligence is capable of destroying the intelligent being he is.

Furthermore, we torment one another with the very nervous intensity of our loves, by trying the impossible, by trying *to be* one another. Loving destroys love.

Worst of all, the very electricity of the torment of loving has destroyed the myth of love.

Sincerely yours,

William A. Boyd
696 Rodman Street
Fredericton, N.B.

Outside, the young men roar on their motorcycles, offending me, because it is spring.

When Tennie comes to complain about my note, he comes as quickly and as viciously as an insinuation. He is at my door before I know it, rapping it vigorously as if to show off his strength of character.

"Yes?" I say, admitting him.

"Bill," he begins, " . . . about this note you sent us . . . "

I think: about the note I sent *you*.

He holds the note out for me to see. I look at it, and then at him, as if trying to connect the two. I notice that somehow or other the note has been crumpled into a ball and then flattened out—unsuccessfully, of course.

"Bill," he begins, and then begins again. "Bill—you can't be serious about this."

"I am."

"Bill, look, I'm sorry. But this must be against the law." He looks at me with that oddly surprised look of a man who has been surprised by death. As, for example, "The German soldier looked as if someone had played a nasty and shocking trick upon him; he clutched at the hole which was appearing in his chest, screamed, and died." I am not sure of the source of that quotation.

"I do not believe there is any law," I say.

"Bill, there must be. You can't raise my rent by $99—just like that! You have to give me notice!"

I am pleased to inform him that I have given him prior notification—the very notice which he holds crumpled in his hand.

"You can't be serious," he says again. "There must be a law."

All of this becomes tiresome.

"There is a law," I inform him. "The law of economics and the avaricious landlord. I invoke the law in my favour. I am the King."

Baffled and uneasy as an animal at bay, Tennie tries to change the direction of discussion. His voice is very loud, and he has not even closed the door.

"Jesus, Bill!" he shouts. I think of a man being beside himself with grief or fury, and I see two of tall Tennie Cord, side by *side,* both six feet five.

"Don't you ever get dressed?" he yells at me.

"I came into this world naked, and I am going out naked. Indeed, I am wearing a hat."

The insolence of my demeanour throws him deeper into his insane fury. I consider the possibility that he may take his fists to me and, moving quickly through the world of wit, I catch him on the rise.

"You were the one who told me how she likes it."

"Likes it?" He is dazzled and desperate, paralysed.

"Yes."

"You're crazy as bugs."

"When is Corrie going to divorce you?"

"Oh, go to hell."

"Here or in the States? It is easier in the States. The land of the opportunity, the home of the free and the brave and the quickie divorce so you can go on loving as you go to supper." Perhaps I am not quite so loquacious as that.

"You're crazier than bugs," he says again.

"If necessary, of course, I shall testify that you beat her."

"Go to hell, Bill Boyd."

"I've heard you. I know that she is going to divorce you. *I know what she wants.*"

"Go to hell."

"Why don't you try violence with me—eh, Tennie? Want to smash up my furniture a little?"

He says nothing.

I demonstrate. I take one of my chairs, one of my beautiful chairs, rubbed down with oil only that morning, take one of my beautiful chairs—look what this man has *created in me!* — I take it, heft it over my head, and smash it on the floor.

It would appear that I am in tears of rage.

In the end I take even my lovely spool-frame sofa, raise it high, and bring it down on the floor. Tennie is leaving. He has caused me to break its lovely back. Can you imagine a dancer — a ballerina — lying in the centre of the stage with her back broken?

Corrie says: "What have we done to you, Bill Boyd, what have we done?"

"Nothing. No — it's true enough — nothing, really." I admit that my nerves are ragged.

She says: "I'm sorry. I'm sorry for all the evil we have brought." And then she looks at me with tears in her eyes. "You are so beautiful."

Should I tell her that the word is wrong — that men are handsome, but women are beautiful, as she is?

No, she says that I do not understand. "You are beautiful," she says.

Uncomprehendingly, I say: "I love you." Does she know what supreme effort that costs me? Does she know that I may never recover from the effect of saying that?

"I love you, too," she says. And no, no that's all wrong. Because if you say "too", then you are merely *reacting*. Merely joining in; merely adding on a *shared courtesy.*

"I love you."

"I love you."

It is better, much better. And she says, "Talk to me?"

"What shall I say?"

"Whatever comes into your head."

"If all things were possible, my beloved, if all things were possible, we would start over from the beginning as if there were nothing but the beginning."

"Of course."

"We may, you know. Can we pay the price?"

"Of course."

"You have beautiful hair."

"Do you like it?"

"Yes."

She grins at me mischievously. "Want to play with it?"

For an answer I take it in my hands, and pull it close to her head; draw her close to me. "It's lovely," I say.

"It's all yours."

"And?" I grin.

"And everything else."

But—ah!—we cannot continue the mood. There are things to be discussed, *will* be discussed, *must* be discussed. The world must have its due, and be dealt with in due course.

"What about Tennie?"

"He'll make do." She laughs. "I'm afraid he'll *have* to."

"Why is it that lovers always talk about the betrayed?"

"Because they cannot talk to one another because . . . "

"Because?"

"Because they *are* one another. It is like talking to oneself!"

"I've talked to you by talking to myself."

"Have you?"

"Umhmm. Over there. While Robert was napping sometimes I talked to you for hours—in the kitchen."

"I heard," I laugh. "I've talked to you, too."

"I've heard," she laughs.

"I love you."

"I love you."

"We love us."

Laughter.

My stomach hurts. I have not eaten all day, wondering, fearing, what Tennie might do. When she tells him how we've talked and loved—surely, surely he will come over here to take his fists to me. And I'm unable — how difficult it is to say it — I'm *unable* to retaliate. I shall have to endure, and survive with cunning.

The ethical situation is complicated. My love is depriving three children of their mother, and a man of his wife and cook. But my love is tearing up my insides.

Dear Sir:

Much, much, much has been written lately about the problems of education. As an ex-teacher myself, freed from the usual drudgery by the fortunate, fateful occurrence of an independent income, perhaps I am qualified to speak to the point.

The first problem of education is, of course, that nobody wishes to pay for it. If teachers were properly paid — if they were paid, and valued, as executives of the large corporations are, if they were given time to think, read, and teach, and given clerical assistance to free them from housekeeping chores, the level of education in this or any other province would immediately be raised. Of course, as any veteran teacher will tell you, you can't make a silk purse out of a sow's ear. You're going to have to give up this foolish belief that *everyone* can be improved by education. (To advance such a theory, if I may say so, is to advance Lamarck's discredited theories on evolution over the proven ones of Charles Darwin.) And indeed, to expand somewhat upon the point, our entire education system is aimed merely at producing little workers for the industrial civilization (capitalist or communist, it doesn't matter, for both are dedicated to industrialism), when in fact we should be attempting to return to a pre-industrial civilization. We must alter our culture.

But much could be done if only we would abandon the idea that "expressiveness" is a good in itself.

"Teach them to express themselves", "Allow them to express themselves" — we hear this kind of cant, day in and day out, as if expressiveness in itself were of proven *worth.* To the contrary, *what* is expressed is far more important. They must learn. They must memorize things. Know facts. If you do not know facts, you know *nothing.* What do you express then but your own empty windiness?

And certainly teachers must learn, and promulgate, something about ethics. It would seem that it is now fashionable to discredit Christianity, and if that is lamentable, it is none the less understandable. Our ideals are Christian; our practices are selfishly commercial, and one after another the Christian sects have invited the money-changers into the temple. Therefore we make wars for commercial profit while proclaiming the love of Christ.

But even if one grants the failures of Christianity, which *I do not, no, not for one moment,* then it remains that ethical decisions must still be made.

Every man is tempted at some time or other to commit murder, as a nation is tempted to commit war. Every man lusts after the women who now so openly display their attractions. And with every impulse of the animal which is in man, there comes the necessity of making a *decision.* Man must *decide.*

To love, for example, is to hurt someone. To love a woman is to hurt her other lovers. To marry a woman is to leave one's parents and hurt them. Yet the Bible insists that this be done.

But it is not done lightly. Pain is *necessary.* A man without pain is not ethically alive.

Decisions must be made, and they must be made within the contexts of the human situation, whether God exists or whether He does not. *He does.*

Decisions must be made to *reject things*. To say NO in THUNDER.

Children must be taught to say NO. Not yes. To say NO.

If our teachers would learn to teach our children to say NO, the nation would be purer for it—purified as by a Holy War. Physical and moral pollution would cease.

Canada was founded as a nation which said NO! to the everlasting "Yes, MORE" of the U.S.A. And look where their practices have led them!

We must say NO.

Sincerely yours,

William A. Boyd
696 Rodman Street
Fredericton, N.B.

They will never print that one—unless they emasculate it with dots, so that it comes out snivelling and carping. They never have the courage to print the courageous letters. They prefer only the little squeaks of the yea-saying liberals, who do not know the pain which adultery brings upon the world. That my love for Corrie will destroy Tennie, and warp forever Alisha, Jack, and Robert, that Tennie will teach the children to remember their mother as "that whore". Ali because I ache to have Corrie forever between the sheets of my bed, heavily laden with the hot, perfumed love of our animal copulation.

I am emptied. Empty. Like Christ after all these crucified centuries, I feel that I have been drunk up forever.

Christ is body.

God is measureless spirit.

I beg of you.

Eight

"Oh, Corrie, hold me, hold me, hold me!"
"Bill!"

The vernal season would seem to have taken hold. Springtime is in full flood and most of it seems to be in my basement. But the birds sing, uncaring.

In the basement I can hear Tennie sloshing about, trying to save the washing machine and dryer. He seems to be swearing at me, although Corrie tries to shush him.

"Did that sonofabitch care if *we* heard *him*?" he says, loudly.

I seem to be out of food. When I look at the shelves in my

kitchen, I see that I should have painted them. Bare, barer, barest.

Empty, discarded cans flow out from beneath the sink at me. Indeed, the door to that area beneath the sink—the trash can is in there somewhere—will not close, for some reason. Perhaps it is blocked by an empty sardine can from Black's Harbour, New Brunswick. Its odour is distinctive. Perhaps there is a squishy banana skin fouling the hinge.

Dear Sir:

Although it is unlikely that you know anything about it—or me, either, for that matter—allow me to leave this little note for posterity.

William A. Boyd, teacher, of 696 Rodman Street, Fredericton, passed away at Victoria Public Hospital on——

Or perhaps: the body of William A. Boyd, a former teacher who retired to live upon his income-property, was found today by some passing children. They said they broke in because of the smell. Investigation by the Fredericton City Police indicated that Boyd had been dead for several days. By the time his body was found he was little more than a pool of oil.

William A. Boyd is survived by no one whatever.

His mother predeceased him by several years. (She died in Clifton, Ohio, on February 22, 1951.)

He was once married to the former Katherine Dobbs, also of Clifton. She is now no more to him than a slab of meat, and in fact remains in his memory chiefly as a lump of head-cheese. She proved to be spiritually faithless, and divorced Boyd after only a few weeks of marriage. The marriage was consummated twenty-one times, and failed on each occasion.

He leaves neither issue nor mourners.

In his last year, Boyd was a prodigious writer of letters to the editors of various newspapers across Canada. He corresponded, as well, with the offices of several politicians, and his name was not unknown in the inner sancta of Washington, Ottawa, London, and even Moscow. He was well-known for his idiosyncratic logic, with which he lashed the mulish public consciousness for its own good.

"You must understand," wrote Boyd, "that the only profundities available to mankind are the rather obvious ones. There's little which is new under the sun, but man has forgotten how to *see* by the light of the sun. Artificial electric light has blinded man to himself and to his nature — as well as to Nature in a larger sense. I simply wanted to make people look at themselves, and see that they, *men*, are animals bent on suicide, if only they will realize it.

"Man is condemned to be human," continued Boyd, but who is going to notice that? All of us, if we admit it, are so *accustomed* to our occupations that we merely trudge away to death — for the sake of an industrial civilization — fittingly, as if on a treadmill.

But a man, I aver, contains *everything he is* and *everyone he has met*. He is what he must necessarily be and he is also what he merely happens to be. I am the owner of a house and a writer of letters, a philosopher.

I am faced daily with the problems of my tenants. For example, Tennie forgets to put out his garbage on the appointed Monday, and on Tuesday he arrives at my door with a bulging green garbage sack in his hand to ask, please, if he can put *his* garbage in *my* can. Of course I agree. I am condemned to be his neighbour. (As Canada is condemned to be the neighbour of the United States.) And my cans are rarely full, even with his additions. Corrie watches his progress from their window, smiling. When Tennie turns to leave, I give her a little wave, and she scurries away, giggling.

Faced with such facts — and faced with a world which seems determined to ignore even the simplest of facts — I have turned my attention to VIRTUE. Does anyone any longer dare to use that word, or to write it in capitals? VIRTUE. How we hunt for systems of government, for drugs, or gadgets, or gimmicks, so that we shall not need to be GOOD.

The real Virtues are in fact very few. And aside from these few Virtues, there is nothing but dancing—dancing as the flowers grow in the rain but to die: polite and sweet, but not human. The human worth is the only worth.

In fact, there are only two real Virtues, I believe: Courage and Endurance. And if we consider Endurance to be a part of Courage, then there is only one. Man faces the awful confusion of the universe and his fellow man, and has the courage to live until he dies.

Virtue, for example, is merely the standing up in the face of a general falling down. My house at 696 Rodman Street shakes and tumbles—admittedly so gradually that you—who do not own it—would not notice it. Who notices an earthquake who is not a part of it?

Tennie tells me it is a good house, basically. It simply needs a good deal of work, and that, he points out, requires something in the way of substantial capital or at least an adequate, assured income. Indeed, *he would say that*!

I stand up to my falling house; I stand up to Tennie. The only difficulty is that man is a rational animal, and is therefore well aware that he is going to die. This makes Virtue all the more difficult, because it cannot be accidental. But the fact that man is rational makes even the most courageous man nervous.

Katherine was afraid of dying, you know. Afraid of even being aware of death. That's why she wouldn't have children—children would remind her of time and passing youth—hers and theirs—and that would remind her of Death. Therefore when I came to her in the bedroom she would sit on the edge of the bed in tears and beg me not to make her pregnant, while I stood beside her, clad ridiculously in pajamas. She insisted that I wear pajamas to bed; that is why I do not wear them now.

None the less, the question before *this house*, the question upon which *this house* must debate and decide before rising for the recess, is this: to fight or not to fight. The enemies of life are everywhere. At our borders, clearly enough, although not only there. Also *within* our borders. Even within our houses and within ourselves. Gentlemen: I put it to you: there is really no need to debate: WE MUST FIGHT.

TO ARMS! Take your rifles in your hands and take to the woods. There snipe at the passing convoys of American troops which are snaking into the interior. Retreat, hide, and come out only at night with a large knife flashing in your hand. The Americans are coming. *We* are coming North to despoil the land with our greed for a *spacious luxury*.

Destroy all automobiles. Ride horses.

Sabotage all oil refineries, oil wells, and paper mills.

DESTROY THE EMPIRE OF ESSO! ANNIHILATE THE ARMIES OF GENERAL MOTORS!

This is good advice, gentlemen, and I beg you to follow it—upon the pain of your own deaths. I shall tell you a joke to help you on your way. On the gallows the condemned man was told by his executioner: "You are going to die." To this the condemned man replied: "So are you."

Therefore I tell you that all this is good advice, although you may think it comes from a madman and a liar. The burden of proof is upon you, my friends. If you judge me guilty you must condemn me. You say the sentence is death? What sentence is not, my learned friends?

I sometimes feel as if I were drifting off to sleep in a deep warm bed, and all the tangled thoughts are nothing but the beginnings of dreams. And have not all of you dreamed, gentlemen? To deny me, gentlemen, is to deny your own dreams. Have you the courage to do that? I thought not. You are cowards all, all.

Right now, at this moment, I am standing at the window of my house at 696 Rodman Street, my typewriter on top of two orange-crates from Tingley's Supermarket, stacked one on top of the other. I am looking out at Rodman Street, and I see that there is a large, orange Allied moving-van backed up to the doorway of the other part of this house—that part usually designated by the postal authorities as 698 Rodman Street. From the door of 698 Rodman Street there issues, at regular intervals, either Professor Harrison (Tennie) Cord or one of his children: Alisha Cord, aged eleven, Jack Cord, aged nine, or young Robert, barely five, who is always in the way. Robert wants to help, of course, while the other two hang back—but there is the danger that Robert might hurt himself, or worse, that he might trip one of the burly moving-men, and cause a great clatter and smashing of crockery. The moving-men smile at him, however, and of course they are so genial because young Robert is being held firmly in hand by the beautiful Corrie Cord, who is standing a little to one side—dressed as always (I think) in blue jeans and sweatshirt. From time to time she holds the door open.

Indeed, the beautiful, blooming Corrie seems to participate even less in her family's moving out than I would have expected. Is it possible—of course it is possible— that she is pregnant? It's an interesting thought to consider, and if you think my previous ethical questions have been tricky, think on this one for a while. This one involves the fruits of love: see the child bursting forth from her, like the slow explosion of a snake from the slime?

Dynamite in the swamp, on a summer day, when the green flies are busy.

Love is GOOD; Marriage is GOOD. When these two Virtues conflict there can only be anxiety and confusion.

It is not fair to confuse people like that. The choice between good and evil is comparatively simple. I see Corrie and Tennie crossed on a shield of honour, both holding axes in their hands, ribbons floating from their naked bodies, and on the ribbons is written something which I cannot make out.

Tennie, dutifully, comes to my door. He has spoken to Corrie, and comes with the stolid attitude of a man who must deal with something which is not joyful. He comes into my living-room and of course I serve him coffee. We must stand up to drink it, naturally, holding the saucers in our left hands and sipping from the cups which we hold in our right hands. It is hot. All of the furniture is smashed. We make awkward jokes about the shambles of our lives. I remark apologetically that I'm afraid that there is no place to sit, and Tennie, shaking his head, says that it is remarkable that I am still able to serve coffee. I say that although it makes me nervous (Corrie would get a smile out of that—I drink twenty cups a day), it is none the less the food of my life, such as it is. I love secret jokes.

I consider the knife in my belt, good for cutting the throats of fat hogs on market day, under the bright sun: the squeal, the gush of blood, the drainage of the animal.

The children are dancing around, first here, then there—eager to get on with it, move on, find a new adventure, become grown-ups and mature and be free: *i.e.*, control their own destinies. Laugh. To be free is to be responsible for one's own failures.

Tennie is embarrassed, shuffling in my broken living-room. Alisha has just said something under her breath to Jack, who has reacted with a loud "Jesus Christ".

Tennie says, laconically, "It's hell to hear oneself echoed by one's children."

I do not appear to understand, and he continues—"That intonation, that expression of Jack's—that's mine, you know." Of course it is. Does he think his life has no results?

You father children and look what you get back: distorted little shaving-mirrors of yourself. It must be uncomfortable. In my mirror I see the dark chin which I scrape with the assistance of Mr. Gillette's invention, Gillette Foamy (Regular) Shaving Cream. I find that one can lasts me over a year. It's a good bargain.

Tennie says: "I feel old," and I cackle.

I ask him about divorce lawyers in the place where he will be going, and he avoids the question by saying that he has had no experience. He doesn't know the procedures.

Perversely, I decide not to enlighten him. That was what he was hinting for – he wants to learn from my experience.

"Well," he says, "I guess they probably send up some kind of notification, and if the party in question does not show up to contest the divorce, the divorce is probably granted."

To stay in Canada is to be guilty of desertion. He is returning south, then.

He talks to me about the divorce procedures in the American states. He has never bothered to learn the Canadian procedures, I see. "I guess it depends on where you live," he asserts.

He is not looking me in the eye.

They are gathered in wealthy rooms, panelled with learned books of the law, a panoply of small idiocies, shifts, and snivellings. Corrie and Tennie sit discreetly apart from one another at opposite corners of the lawyer's massive desk, which is piled high with papers. The lawyer wears rimless glasses, but he is a messy man none the less. He is merely marching through well-trained steps and collecting a fat fee. He's very proud of himself; he's a fat man.

As the big moving-men march into the nearly loaded moving-van, I notice that it shakes under their tread and waddles in its squat.

Does he wonder if I can take care of her?

Tennie is infuriating in the questions which he poses

without actually asking. Why doesn't he come right out and say: "Look, I've been rather fond of the woman for a few years now, I've had her so many times I cannot count them, fathered three children on her, and know secrets about her which you won't know for ten years, if ever. Are you sure you are capable of looking after her?"

I take all this as a kind of chaffing pleasantry. He sounds like a worried father, giving away his daughter to a ne'er-do-well.

Of course, there are certain things which *I* refuse to say, like: "Are you sure you'll get the divorce, that you won't leave us living in sin?"

But I'll tell you why I don't ask things like that. Because high and mighty Tennie would blow into one of his insane rages and invoke the name of Christ in his most habitual curse (you will have noticed—have you noticed?—how habitually and meaninglessly he speaks of Christ?) and say something like: "I'm the man of honour in this affair. You're not, goddamn you. Get your face out of the honourable concerns and leave the honour to me!"

He goes off to help the moving-men carry out his goods, his record-player, and his books (it seems that he is taking *everything* he can lay his hands on), and they are not particularly pleased with his help because they have to stop every now and then and tell him where to put things in the van or, worse, re-arrange what he has already put down in his clumsy and glamorous fashion.

I point out all this to Corrie when I stroll outside to watch, and she agrees that Tennie is a man who is unsure of what he wants, but she defends him in her way: "He always likes to be helpful, if he can," she says, a little sadly. Things are breaking up. I return to my house to watch.

My house is falling down; I am ageing. Old people live in old houses where the gardens have overgrown into cancers. The sunflowers, the lilac bushes, the roses, run riot and encroach upon the house, smothering it in their heavy perfume. The air tastes green, and old, like the earth in the cellar, slimy to the touch like the inside of the rain-barrel where we have feared. The trellis, attached to the side of the house for years, is pulling away. The apple tree is bent over with liver-spotted apples bent onto the ground, rotting even as they grow.

It has struck me, ladies and gentlemen, that much of our present agony could be spared if only we could dispose of the monetary system. I do not mean that we ought to reform it—such half-measures merely maintain the essential *status quo,* and I want to retreat pell-mell, run away to fight again another day.

No, we ought to do away with money altogether. We ought to be paid in kind (do you know the origin of that expression—*Kine*—Kind?) for the work which we do. For example, we ought to be given houses in return for our labours. As long as we are satisfactory workers we retain the house. When we retire, we have a house. Should the house wear out before the man, then he will receive a new house, suitable for his purposes. Thus an ageing man need not live in an old house, nor, for that matter, must a young man live in some raw new development.

There is no sense whatever in having old people in large, empty houses. People so old that they cannot remember the back room except as it was in their childhood, when they hid there in fear. Now they squint going into the smelly darkness of each room; they have ceased to turn on lights because it makes no difference any more. They can no longer distinguish between the old smell of apple-sauce in the dining-room and the smell of stale old beds in the bedrooms. All are one. If you come across one of these old people sitting by his ancient dining-room table, doubtless varnished oak, you would perceive nothing more than a strange white shadow. You might think it a ghost until you saw it move, and perceived its substance. The white object is like nothing so much as a giant slug, there in the moist darkness.

Will Corrie and I be happy together? I have no doubt but that we shall. Of course, we shall have to adjust to one another, and that is never an easy job, I'm told, even at the best of times and under the best of circumstances. Indeed, Katherine and I never made it, did we? She merely flitted away.

But we shall get by. In order to support her and pay hush-money to Tennie for the support of the children, I shall, of course, have to get a job. My idyllic existence as a man of property, as a lord living on the income of his estates, has come to the end.

But singleness is, of course, a philosophic error. The lonely man, it is true, is troubled only by his loneliness. But a man like that is incomplete. He is eunuch, odd, perhaps queer? Standing alone in his solitary majesty or damn foolishness, fearful of his own mortality.

One achieves immortality only by coupling with the hot body of a woman. So be it. It is determined, yea, preordained by God. I go forth —

I go forth to get a job. Corrie and I hold long discussions about this. At first I hold out, suggesting that I do a bit of "supply-teaching". That, with the rent from the other side, will provide enough, I believe. But Corrie says that no, she won't allow that. "You hated teaching, didn't you?" And that's true, I admit. She argues further that there is nothing in the *temporary* life for one in search of immortality.

She asks me as she goes to bed, shrugging off her peignoir to fall about her ankles, standing there alive, damp, she asks me: "Do you want to be immortal?"

I do, I do, Oh, I do.

But when I fail to find suitable employment, Corrie is vexed.

It is the natural biology of a woman to think in terms of

her nest. We should not be hard on women for demanding so much of their spouses. It is the woman's function to survive and reproduce, and this controls their thinking. Food is the mother of their philosophy — not airy hopes and ideals.

It comes to this. She says to me: "We may have to give up the house, Bill."

I pretend not to have heard her, and she repeats the awful statement. "We may have to give up the house." I look out the window at the bright, warm day, pretending not to hear. How incredibly green everything is. The ground riots with growth.

Should I have remonstrated? Should I have shouted "Never!" No, it doesn't pay to be melodramatic. It gets you nowhere. My mother always said: "Don't show off — you don't win anything that way and you get a lot of enemies." Like so many things which she said to me, things which are imprinted on my mind as surely and securely as the ten commandments, there's a lot of truth in that. It is good advice. But whoever was content with good advice? Good advice *tightens one in.* In response to Corrie's suggestion, I merely grunt.

But she whines: "We have to have *money.*"

What am I to reply to that? I kiss her to make it all right, and she turns away from me, angrily. "Kissing won't help," she says, and I am reminded of the old adage which is engraved on varnished plaques of pine from Coral Gables, Regina, and Wisconsin Dells: "Kissing don't last; Cooking do."

"Bill," she says. "I'm sorry, but we have to be practical. We have to *live.*" I relent — she is so beautiful, so tender and rich in her warm skin, tanned to a deep brown by the long summer sun. I have put a high fence around the yard, and now she goes back there to stretch out on the reclining lawn-chair, wearing only her skimpy polka-dot bikini. I come out to look at her and find her oily with sweat and sleepy from the sun. She says to me lazily that she never got a tan like this in the States. I tell her that it is due to the long days, and she, reminded that she has all this time on her hands because she has lost her children forever, forever (weeping), becomes distraught. In the old days — once upon a time — I would then have brought her smelling salts and guided her into a place in the shade. Now I must be more modern. I take her into the house, remove her bikini, and put her in the shower, where I wash her lovely body, very humbly. "Oh, Bill — my children!" But she recovers from her tears.

She is very well-tanned. "The fact remains," she says, "we have to have money to live, and we can't live off the rent from the other side — and we haven't even rented it yet." I remind her that it will not be difficult in the autumn, when the new faculty arrives, desperate for housing.

I should not have said that. Her smile is ironic.

She adds up the figures for me. She says: "You sit down there at the kitchen table, and let me do some figuring." I obey.

She makes a list.

Mortgage payments to Secombe	$108/mo.
Tax	450/yr.
Food (estimated)	200/mo.

Income:

(she puts this on the left, I suppose, because my house is on the left side.)

$0

The dollar sign is one of the ugliest things Canada ever imported from the United States. The thin end of the wedge.

"But look," she says, "I have an idea." She is pretending that a thought has just occurred to her. I am not fooled. She has been working on something, on *me.*

"Just for instance," she says, "just for instance, we might give up the house." She looks at me. "Grant me just the 'for instance'."

"All right," I say.

"O.K. We sell the house at a pretty good profit—it shouldn't be hard."

"It wouldn't be—but I've never thought of it."

"Then," she says, "we might go some place where the cost of living is cheaper."

"And where might that be?"

"St. Martin's."

"St. Martin's? It's down on the coast. Nearly deserted."

"It's beautiful," she says. She has been down there on one of the Cord family outings, all the children and Tennie piled into the big, dirty old VW bus, going out laughing with baskets of food and toys to keep Robert amused. "The tourists would come, and we could have a little house and"—she smiles at me, hopefully—"open a restaurant."

"A restaurant."

She is really quite excited by the idea. I believe she foresees a little whitewashed cottage with a red-tiled roof and a surprising number of cozy little rooms upstairs where we shall live, and downstairs there will be a kitchen and a large, L-shaped, panelled room with beams and pewter tankards hanging from nails on the wall. Brass warming-pans and the like. Trivets everywhere with little copper kettles and teapots sitting on them. It is useless to tell her that we'd never get a liquor licence. She would argue that of course we would—it would be for the *tourists*. New Brunswick needs tourists.

Because she has already run ahead in her imagination, she sees me as the genial, beaming host and herself as the surprisingly young and beautiful wife, attending on the customers.

"We could have a different menu every day," she says. "And I could do the cooking and you could look after the bar."

Me. An ex-schoolteacher become a publican with a fat belly and a white apron, washing glasses, greasy from the tourists' fat fingerprints.

"For example," she continues, "on Mondays we could have lobster Newburg, with side dishes like fiddleheads and New Brunswick potatoes – I'll serve *hash-brown*," she exclaims. "They'll love them. Don't you see – we'll break the usual restaurant menu, and people will be *glad* to drive a few miles to reach us. On Tuesdays we'll have salmon, and on Wednesdays, trout, and on Thursdays we'll have a special spaghetti at a low price and special prices for drinks and on Friday, a smorgasbord. We'll be *rich*," she shouts.

All of this is making me hungry. I have a sudden desire for scalloped potatoes.

"No," I say.

She runs in tears to our room to flop on the huge bed which I have just purchased. "Oh, Jesus, Jesus, Bill, won't you ever see *sense*?" Her great brown eyes are turned up at me, full of tears.

If I do not do as she wants me to do – then I am not a sensible man.

I am insulted by this because I *am* a sensible man, and I stalk off. To hell with her. To hell with everyone and everything. I'll commit suicide and get out of the whole mess. To hell with her and Tennie and her three children and the house and everything. Let her go back to that fool, Tennie!

Then, as I sit in the cool living-room, out of the sun, she comes and puts her arms around me and begins to kiss my neck quickly and softly, tickling me.

You see – don't you – that Corrie, like most women,

thinks that love, just the fact of love, makes everything all right. It doesn't matter that life has gone from bad to worse, that the universe is breaking down like an old man with night-time sweats, that there is war nearly everywhere and anarchy nearly everywhere there isn't a war. Life has become tawdry. Our restaurant in St. Martin's! It would be tawdry. What about a Hamburger Heaven with the glass front full of cut-outs of hamburgers and french fries and sodas and ice-cream — all fading in the sun and the flies buzzing around. Hail to Dairy Queen: the New Monarch.

Corrie thinks that love is the answer to everything. "Oh, Bill," she wails, "if only you love me everything will be all right."

Will it, I ask you? Love doesn't feed hungry people. We need heavy industry for that.

"Oh, Bill," she cries, and locks her arms around my neck. "Give me a baby and I'll be happy." Like a child saying, "Buy me an ice-cream cone and I'll never, never, never, ask for anything again."

"Oh, Bill," she is with me in the kitchen, her arms around me, her head pressed into my shoulder. "Say you love me."

"I love you."

And then everything is all right, I suppose.

But suppose we must have the children with us? Suppose Tennie remarries and decides to ship the kiddies back to their mother and their new father? He's perfectly capable of doing a thing like that, of taking a woman to wife, heedless of the consequences, just for spite. Believe me! People have married with less reason! And then the kids are shipped back to me. Alisha and Jack have the vulgar mouths they have developed at their parents' knees, and it is a well-known fact that young Robert dislikes me with a persevering perversity.

And would you listen to the racket they make! Their everlasting yammer, yammer, yowl. Gimme, gimme, and

Mine, and "He *hit* me." The outrages which seem to be constant; the totally uncivilized society of the untamed savages. They thunder through the house, yelling at one another. "That's *mine*," and "Mother, can I have a . . . ?" and "Mother, can I have a . . . ?"

No.

Why not?

It is their unshakable belief that they deserve everything, and justice is to be found only—just possibly—in the reasons for our inability to give them *everything*.

But I *want* it.

Well, so do I, you little brats. So do *I*.

They look at me as if they want to kill me, and quite possibly they do. I am afraid to allow that sweetly smelling Alisha to bring me a cup of coffee. She's after her mother *already*, mind you, to buy her a brassiere. And why? Because she bounces and flops? Not at all. No evidence of anything like that yet: she can still wear a T-shirt and there's not so much as a pinch of nipple showing. No bosom yet; still less breast; no hint of an udder. But because *all the other girls wear them*.

I have not been listening at the wall for the past year without learning *some*thing!

Jack has simply turned sullen and uncommunicative, but delights in making as much noise as possible when he comes down the stairs. If he thinks he can get away with it, he jumps the last four or five steps in order to land with an assertive crash at the bottom.

Now look here, young man, what have you been told about that?

His look is helpless. "I forgot."

"That's a fact but it is not an excuse."

He turns sullen. What am I to do? Turn to Corrie? She throws up her hands and says, quite satisfied with herself: "I can't cope with the little monsters."

"Then take to the gin bottle!" I shout. "Because that's the next step!"

We have some hellish arguments. She has no self-discipline whatever, that woman.

"Do you want me to leave?"

"No, no. No, not that. But can't you make them be a little more quiet?"

"Oh, please, Bill. They're *kids*. Kids make noise."

When they tear through the house I shudder. Their everlasting racket makes my nerves twitch, and I find myself developing a tic in my shoulder muscles from them.

And I am thwarted at every turn. I try to explain something, and my explanation is dismissed as if it were of no account. *Any* statement from *any*body or *any* source is sufficient to repudiate me.

We were arguing about fluoridation the other day. It has been voted down, democratically, here in Fredericton, and Corrie is in a rage. "None of these people *care* if the children's teeth rot."

"The children ought to brush their teeth properly, with salt if necessary. The people here simply do not want to put chemicals in the water supply because it might turn out to be dangerous."

"But Bill, they're doing it *every*where. It *does* prevent cavities."

"At what cost?"

"But all those dentists can't be wrong!"

"Of course they can. They're as stupid as everyone else."

"Do *you* know any better? Are you a dentist?" She has that crazy glint in her eye as if I'm about to spring another surprise on her and admit that yes, I practised dentistry for three years in Arkansas. My lies make her uneasy, but I keep her in love with me with them—trying to find the bottom, the absolute truth which is within me.

"I know enough to know when I don't know enough."

"Jesus, Bill."

"There *are* doctors and dentists who are against it."

"Cranks."

"Am *I* a crank, then?"

She does not answer. I demand an answer, but she does not respond. She knows enough to shut up when she's ahead. I get out my stack of clippings and show her a letter to the editor of the Fredericton *Daily Gleaner* by Dr. K. A. Baird.

"There," I say. "He's a doctor."

"I'm tired. Oh boy, am I tired!"

"You should go to bed earlier."

She is screaming at me. "I hate you, I hate you, I hate you. Can't you *ever* stop thinking?"

Of course, my dear Corrie. When I am dead.

Fluoridation is the perfect example of the too-hasty invocation of a liberal scientific theory. It is, in fact, anti-empirical in its methods. Before it has been tested on sufficient generations to indicate *any*thing about its long-term effects –

"They've studied rats."

"We're humans."

"Rats prove –"

"Not at all," I counter. "Remember the thalidomide babies? Thalidomide was tested on rats. It turned out that women were more sensitive to thalidomide than rats."

"You want me to stop taking the pill?" she screams.

No, no. I do not want that.

"Fluoridation," she says, stalking off. "Fluoridation. How can *anyone* in his right mind be against fluoridation?"

You see? She did not bother to listen to what I said. What she had read in *Time* magazine and the *Star Weekly* was enough for her. All the liberal scientists were on the side of fluoridation; only us old doubters were on the other. We count for nothing.

Surely the same thing was thought, gentlemen, when the

internal combustion engine was designed. And we thought that oil was a great boon to mankind. We thought that oil brought riches.

Count the number and effect of the mistakes with oil in the past couple of years. Chedabucto Bay in Nova Scotia, Athabasca, the Gulf of Mexico, the beaches at Santa Barbara, and the wreck of the *Torrey Canyon*. The St. Croix "mistake"; the "mistake" on the Miramichi.

Oh, yes. Add that up. And add up the effect of those other boons, DDT and 2-4-5-D, while we're at it.

You see, don't you, that the papal courts were right in dealing with Galileo. The fact that he was accurate and correct in his observations is beside the point. He was unwise; he was wrong for the happiness of mankind. And that is what counts. I would remind you, also, that the Russian biologist, Lysenko, was officially recognized as "correct", as are the fluoridationists. Wiggle around *that* for a while.

Man destroys. I conclude that man cannot *help* destroying. Man is a suicidal species, bent on the grandiose gesture of taking everything on the planet down with him in his fall, convinced that he is doing it for his own good and happiness—and for a monstrous great profit while he's at it.

In the bedroom she does not look at me at first. She strips down and peels away her paisley-patterned bikini panties. Her pubic hair is thick. I am struck blind; struck dumb by the heady, heavy perfume of her body.

I am Adam. She bends herself back in the bed like a frog to offer herself to me. My queen. I advance in my brutish love to wallow in her, and I do, grunting in the rich gravy which is Corrie, grunting with the brutish glory of the belief that I am, at last, a King.

Then, rolling over (she rolls over and is asleep immediately), I begin to take stock of how far I have fallen, as if ages had passed since I created this household.

I think, ironically, that my kingdom despairs.

I realize that, like an actor, I have a real secret name which nobody knows. How dark and still it is! I have always hated my name. I am like an author writing under a pseudonym about a character whose name exists only in fiction. And that fiction, in turn, is played on stage and screen by an actor who has a stage-name, and whose real name is, as he knows full well, of doubtful legitimacy.

At these moments of horror—and only at these moments—I am completely honest. I know my real name. And I shall not tell it to you.

To go forth. Gentlemen, it is necessary for me to go forth. I shall board up the windows of 696-698 Rodman Street and write KEEP OUT in slashes of black paint on the boards.

I shall put on my night's costume, carefully preserved—Night's Knight.

Do you know the simplest method of sabotage? Look at me. If you met me on the street you would never see me. I have taken such pains to become ordinary. I eschew all dramatic costumes in favour of the action which is dramatic to *me only*. I am my only audience. Watch me.

You take a simple book of matches, and a package of cigarettes. Nothing could be simpler; nothing could be more easily obtained.

You choose your target. Seldom the obvious one.

You find the ever-present pile of wood-chips, or shavings, or the trash barrel, or a pile of rags. Gasoline or kerosene is seldom necessary. Fires are really quite difficult to trace. If I burned down this house tomorrow, no one would ever know my shame or torment.

You take an ordinary book of matches and a cigarette. You light the cigarette, and take a few puffs.

It is best at closing time. I am thinking of the paper-mills along the beautiful St. John River, owned by the infamous K. C. Irving. Paper is one of our evils, it seems. Perhaps the potato-chip factories. An insult to the palate as well.

I am the new Johnny Appleseed, the unseen Revolutionary, the Cleansing Fire. May God forgive me or reward me.

Surely there is no God to damn me.

Surely.

You see, there is always the principle of the Christian Knight, the man who went forth to exemplify the conduct of Christ. And, when that failed, he killed so that the unbelievers would be less. This was killing invoked for the sake of love. And it is with the principles of the Christian Knight that I am in accord. Mercy. Love. Mercy is the Christian virtue, although it is always dangerous to become a knight for the love of a woman rather than for the love of Christ.

A Baptist is the best argument against Mercy. He neither exemplifies that Virtue nor deserves it. Kill me.

Mercy. I am the Knight, going forth.

In the dead of the night, for the code of gentlemanly conduct, for the love of a good woman, I go forth with my books of matches and my pack of cigarettes. The total investment is less than a dollar.

I go forth. I find my dark shed, the smell of old oil, the foul smell of trash. I light my cigarette.

I learned this trick reading boys' books about World War II. The French used it against the Nazis, I believe. Could you have eliminated my horrible knowledge?

I smoke only a few puffs of the cigarette. You will have noticed that I am not a habitual smoker. And then I take the lighted cigarette and lay it in behind the matches in the book of matches, perpendicular to the matches themselves. I place this simple device (man is a tool-making animal) in a carefully chosen spot. Then I leave.

Who could possibly notice me? I am at best merely a spirit, the worker for salvation in the universe. The evidence destroys itself.

After I am gone there are the gentle beginnings of the crackling fire, warm to the hands, welcome on a frosty evening. How we all gather around the stove, and I always wanted to roast marshmallows. I'm very fond of marshmallows, and catholic in regard to the methods of preparation. Usually I toast them lightly, so that only the outside is browned, and the centre remains chewy and nearly solid. On other occasions I prefer to let them catch fire like a torch, then blow out the fire and pop the charred object into my mouth, burning my tongue.

The fire rages.

Look how tiny those words are. The fire rages. They are hardly more important than ants. Look away from them. You will think of ants.

The fire rages, and there is a roar as if God were approaching through the trees, coming in through the windows as the fire creates its own kind. And all of us, who do not really believe in God, believe in fire.

They are finished loading the big van. The workmen have closed and bolted, and even locked the back doors. Tennie speaks to them, then to Corrie. The children are around them.

Here comes Corrie to my door, at last. I can see her coming, walking slowly. How *tight* her jeans are. The sun is high and lovely, oh lovely. It is finally summer and I want to drink it in, and am offended to find myself considering suicide once again on such a lovely day. My house glows with warmth.

Gentlemen, should I kill her? Should I place my thumbs at the centre of her throat and watch her eyes roll back with horror? I've read that you have to find a certain bone there while she struggles. Have you ever seen a mare, mounted by the stallion for the first time? The eyes rolled back, leaping, frightened? To press that bone, snap it, kill Corrie.

I shall not hold her against her will. When she is before me, smiling as she always does, I say (feigning shyness), "Will you marry me?" and she agrees.